A CASE OF LONE STAR

Kinky Friedman, former leader of the band The Texas Jewboys, lives on a ranch in the Texas Hill Country with six dogs, two cats and one armadillo. He is the author of fourteen and a half internationally acclaimed mystery novels and nine country music albums. These days, he travels the world, singing the songs that made him infamous and reading from the books that made him respectable.

KINKY FRIEDMAN
A Case of Lone Star

Vandam Press
New York, Kerrville, Jerusalem, Honolulu

A CASE OF LONE STAR

A Vandam Press book published by arrangement with the author.

Printing History
This book was first published by
William Morrow and Company in 1987

First Vandam Press printing: August, 2000
Second Vandam Press printing: December 2001

For information contact:
Vandam Press, Inc., Copyrights and Permissions,
Post Office Box 155, Midwood Postal Station, Brooklyn,
New York 11230 USA

The Vandam Press, Inc., website is at:
http://www.vandampress.com

ISBN: 0-9702383-1-2

Vandam Press books are published by Vandam Press, Inc.
The name 'Vandam Press' and the stylized 'V' logo used by
Vandam Press, Inc., are pending trademarks.

2 4 6 8 10 9 7 5 3

Introduction

A Case of Lone Star, my second novel, was begun in New York and completed in Texas. Its setting is the legendary Lone Star Café in Manhattan where I performed for many years, sometimes walking on my knuckles or having to be wheeled onstage on a gurney. The book deals with cats, cocaine, cigars, country music, and anything else that begins with a 'c'. It also deals heavily with the Hillbilly Shakespeare, the Jesus of the Bible Belt, the Anne Frank of the Louisiana Hayride, Hank Williams, who passionately intermingled his life and his work, the latter being beautiful beyond words and music, the former ending officially on January 1, 1953, crucified in a Cadillac on a lost highway at age twenty-nine which was a little younger than Jesus but a little older than John Keats.

The best book I ever read on Hank is *Your Cheatin' Heart* by Chet Flippo. It not only afforded me great background and resource material for writing this book but it also provides the reader with deep, almost uncanny insights into the heart and mind of the greatest country singer who ever lived. In *A Case of Lone Star*, however, we are searching for a crazed serial killer who believes he's Hank Williams. Anyone who's crazy enough to get into country music in the first place probably has a little bit of Hank in his soul, but most of us don't interpret his lyrics quite as literally or quite as diabolically.

The Lone Star Café itself was practically an institution in New York, sometimes bordering on a mental institution. There was enough Irving Berlin's White Christmas around on any given night to decorate a large nativity scene. From the late Seventies until the mid-Eighties I performed there often with a band variously called The Entire Polish Army, The Exxon Brothers, and The Shalom Retirement Village People. Most of the band members have gone to visit Hank by now and I probably would've as well if I hadn't bugged-out for the dug-out and headed back to Texas in 1985. My personal goals at the time were to get off cocaine and finish this book – it's hard to type a book if Bob Marley keeps falling out of your left nostril – both of which I accomplished. My personal goals are now to be fat, famous, financially-fixed, and a faggot by fifty-five. I think that you'll agree that I've met with success in some areas.

As far as the characters in this book are concerned, Detective-Sergeant Mort Cooperman and Detective-Sergeant Buddy Fox, in real life, were the owner and manager of the Lone Star Café. Ratso, Rambam, McGovern, Gunner, Uptown Judy and Downtown Judy continue to walk the streets of New York. I do not mean to imply that any or all of them are male or female prostitutes. It's certainly possible but I do not know this for a fact. Indeed, who among us has never been a prostitute of some kind at some time or other in our lives? Cleve is out of the Pilgrim State Mental Hospital, by the way. The original Lone Star went belly-up in 1989. And Ol' Hank is looking down on the world with his patented crooked smile wondering whatever happened to the lost art of country music.

Speaking of lost art, I'd like to thank Vandam Press for including *A Case of Lone Star* in its new Masters of Crime series. My earlier books are like little lost children to me now. I want them to go out in the world, meet people, make friends, and do well for themselves. On any given night I'm sure that some of them probably hold up better than I do.

Kinky Friedman
November 1, 1999
Oslo, Norway

For Tom Baker
1940–1982

When Irish hearts are happy,
All the world seems bright and gay,
And when Irish eyes are smiling,
Sure they steal your heart away.

Acknowledgments

The author would like to thank the following people for their help and encouragement: Tom Friedman, Earl Buckelew, Dylan Ferrero, Dr Jay Wise and Larry 'Ratso' Sloman; Esther 'Lobster' Newberg at ICM; James Landis, Jane Meara and Lori Ames at Beech Tree Books; and Steven Rambam, technical adviser.

A Case of Lone Star

1

I opened the window and reached for the puppet head on top of the refrigerator. That was where I always kept it. It was once a little Negro puppet that I'd bought at a flea market on Canal Street. Now it was an indispensable part of my life. I had removed the head of the puppet, wedged the key to the front door of the building in its mouth, and attached a colorful, homemade parachute to the whole operation. The front facade of 199B Vandam appeared for all the world to be nothing but an abandoned, gray, graffiti-strewn warehouse, which, in fact, it had once been before somebody got clever and converted the whole building into loft space for people like myself and like Winnie Katz, who ran a lesbian dance class in her studio one floor above me. I listened to the rhythmic thuddings of Winnie's girls starting up over my head, and then I remembered Down-town Judy had been waiting on the sidewalk below. I looked down and she was still there. Getting a little colder maybe, but still there. I threw down the puppet head and closed the window.

It was Thanksgiving in New York, and about the only thing I was thankful for was that I didn't live in New Jersey.

My spacious, wind-swept loft was cold as hell. Maybe colder. It depended on what season it was in hell.

The cat had been hunkered down next to the coffee perco-lator most of the afternoon. It was now almost midnight. I was looking forward to doing a little horizontal mambo with Downtown Judy.

There was Downtown Judy and there was Uptown

3

Judy, and neither knew the other one existed. I liked to keep it that way.

The day had been a typical gray blurry Thursday with damn little going on to get excited about. Earlier that afternoon I'd gotten into an ugly altercation at a vegetarian restaurant on Seventh Avenue over whether the smoke from my cigar was harmful to the patrons eating their bean curds.

That was the high point of the day.

Downtown Judy and I hadn't been in bed long when the phone rang. It cut through the two of us like a shrimping knife. I turned in the general direction of the sound, reached across the darkness, and collared the blower in my left hand.

'Start talkin',' I said.

'Yeah. Hey, man, this is Cleve at the Lone Star.' Cleve was the manager of the club and a friend of mind. He'd started out as a road manager with my band.

'What is it, pal?' I asked. 'I'm right in the middle of someone.'

'I've got a problem over here,' said Cleve.

'What is it? You run out of tube socks for the gift shop?'

'It's a little more serious than that,' said Cleve. 'It's Larry Barkin.' Larry Barkin was an old acquaintance of mine, a good-looking prima donna of a country star I'd known in Nashville back before both of us were nothing. In the past few years he'd sold a lot of records to a lot of lonely housewives. He was currently appearing with his two brothers, Randy and Jim, at the Lone Star. Larry Barkin and the Barkin Brothers.

'What's the matter?' I asked. 'He won't go on for the second show?'

'He won't ever go on again, man,' said Cleve. 'He's dead.'

4

I ankled it over to Hudson Street and nailed a Checker right off the bat, which was lucky because I was beginning to feel like the inside of a Dreamsicle. Being in a warm Checker cab in the New York wintertime is like being back in the womb, even if the womb is hurtling across Fourteenth Street at fifty miles an hour. I wouldn't say that it provided an opportunity to meditate, but if you tried you could almost think.

That's what I was trying to do, but it wasn't really working out. Ever since I'd plucked a beautiful young victim from her would-be mugger at an all-night cash machine in the Village my life as a simple, broken-hearted country singer was over. COUNTRY SINGER PLUCKS VICTIM FROM MUGGER, the headline read at the time. Then with several fortuitous forays into crime-solving in the Village, I'd become a hero to my friends and family. With the help of my friend McGovern, a reporter for the *Daily News*, I'd become good copy. And, with all of this, I'd become a nuisance to the cops of the Sixth Precinct. You can't please everybody.

It was 2.30 in the morning when the cab jerked to a halt at the corner of Fifth Avenue and Thirteenth Street. The Lone Star Cafe. At one time or another, everyone from the Rolling Stones to the Blues Brothers had jammed there. Tonight was a different kind of jam. I paid the cabbie and headed for the revolving door in the front of the place. Cleve was standing there looking fairly cadaverous himself.

'Fox and Cooperman here yet?' I asked. They were two detectives who worked out of the Sixth Precinct, and they liked to try to work me over every chance they got. They didn't like country singers-turned-amateur detectives. Or anybody else.

Cleve shook his head and led me up the back stairs of the Lone Star past the balcony and to the third floor, where the dressing rooms were.

'Let's make it fast, pal,' I told him as he unlocked the door to the third floor. 'This may be the Village, but I don't want to have two dicks leaning on me if I can help it.'

We walked down the narrow hallway of the third floor past walls that were strewn with graffiti – the names of musicians and bands who had played the Lone Star in the past. Some of them were famous now, some of them were dead, and some of them were both. Like Larry Barkin.

Cleve unlocked the door to Barkin's room. I still didn't like dressing rooms. Dressing rooms, amplifiers, booking agents, fans, groupies, coke dealers, bass players from LA – it was enough to make an insurance salesman out of anybody. I'd seen that dressing room when every inch of the floor was soaked in beer and every tabletop was strewn with cocaine. No joy actually. No joy at all.

There wasn't a hell of a lot of joy in the place right now, come to think of it.

Larry Barkin had been an old friend of mine. Old friends are ones you may not really like but you're stuck with because you're old friends. You can pick your friends and you can pick your nose, but you can't wipe your friends off on your saddle.

Whether I'd liked Larry Barkin or not was apparently rather a moot point. He was slumped over a folding chair in the far right corner of the room.

It was a good thing he wouldn't be needing his Gibson guitar anymore because somebody had evidently bashed in the back of his skull with it. The broken guitar was lying on the floor beside the chair. Rusty blood was already doing a nice job of congealing in his straw-blond blow-dried hair. A yellow cowboy shirt with silver sequins picked up light

6

like a miniature Milky Way. Face was a little off-color – California suntan on a sluggish freeway to chartreuse.

Boots by Larry Mahan. Had a pair myself but not quite as nice. 'What are those?' I asked. 'Brontosaurus foreskin?' Cleve said nothing. He was looking at the pink cowboy scarf around Barkin's neck. Whoever had tied it for him had been a trifle overzealous with the job – about seven notches worth.

'Shit,' said Cleve.

'You can say that again,' I said. 'Bashed with his own guitar and then strangled with his own bandanna. Charming.'

Cleve fidgeted nervously. Death will do that to you. It's almost as bad as going onstage.

'Who the hell could've done something like this?' asked Cleve. My eyes lingered for a moment on Barkin's sweet and swollen face.

'Somebody who didn't like his last record,' I said.

I hauled my old snot rag out of my hip pocket and reached across to the breast pocket of Barkin's yellow-fringed cowboy shirt. Something green was sticking up out of the pocket, and it wasn't Kermit the Frog. I took a quick glance at it and I put it right back the way I had found it, just peeping out at me over the top of the pocket. It was a two-dollar bill.

'Curious,' I said.

'What do you make of it?' asked Cleve. I shrugged.

'Two rides on the subway,' I said.

3

From Cleve I was able to obtain a fairly complete list of the people who'd been in the dressing room during the evening. Of the five people he mentioned, one was a beautiful blond

British photographer, one was a mysterious bald-headed lawyer who'd been dispensing cocaine, and three were close, personal friends of mine. With friends like these, I thought, who needed murder suspects?

And then, for all I knew, Randy and Jim could've croaked their more celebrated sibling themselves. These country music family acts had been known to get a little biblical at times. Cain had set the precedent some years back when he'd gone a step beyond mere sibling rivalry and lunched his brother. If this was what had occurred, it was going to make for fairly deep waters, and not the kind that were going to part very easily.

These were the thoughts going through my head when the large, surly form of Detective Sergeant Mort Cooperman blackened the doorway behind me. The snakelike figure of Detective Sergeant Buddy Fox lurked a few steps behind him like an unhealthy shadow. Cooperman's little eyes roamed the little room. They took in the corpse and Cleve and came to a bumpy landing when they reached me.

'Oh, Christ,' he said, 'it's another goddamn case of *déjà vu*!'

'I don't speak Italian,' I said.

I never found talking to cops all that amusing. I told them the little I knew, but clearly I was the wrong person in the wrong place at the wrong time, and they grilled me like a blackened redfish. It made for an unpleasant nightcap to an unpleasant evening.

It was a quarter after who-gives-a-damn when the cabbie dropped me off at the corner of Hudson Street and Vandam. I walked the final couple of blocks to no. 199B.

I took the freight elevator with the one exposed light bulb up to the fourth floor, unlocked the door to my loft, found a cigar and the old bull's horn that I sometimes used for a shot glass. Then I found a handy bottle, poured it into the bull's horn, and discharged it into my mouth like Ernest Hemingway's shotgun. I didn't know if old Ernest had had a cat or a telephone, but I did, and both of them were complaining to me. I walked over and picked up the cat and the blower. The cat hated to be picked up but the blower didn't seem to mind. It said, 'Hi. Where have you been? I've been calling for ages.'

It was Uptown Judy. I looked around the bedroom sort of as an afterthought and noticed that Downtown Judy had apparently vacated the premises. My heart did not skip a beat.

'I've been over at the Lone Star,' I said.

'You're kidding,' she shrilled in my ear. 'That's where I'm calling from, baby.'

I was still holding the bull's horn but I'd deposited the cat on top of the desk.

'That's Mr Baby, to you,' I said.

It was agreed that Uptown Judy would come over to the loft. I hung up the phone, poured another shot, and lit the cigar. Always keeping it well above the flame. My mind was not on the two Judys, however. It was on the two-dollar bill.

Even with inflation, Larry Barkin had gotten more than he'd bargained for.

4

When I woke Friday morning Uptown Judy was already uptown. Nothing too earth-shattering about that. Some people worked for a living. I jumped into the rain-room and took a shower, then stood around in my purple bathrobe slurping a hot cup of coffee, smoking my first cigar of the day, and watching the garbage trucks moving in slow motion through the freezing drizzle that was slanting down onto the world below. The old rusty fire escapes were still there across the street. They weren't much prettier than the garbage trucks but they were quieter. Vandam Street was a major garbage-truck staging area for the city. Nonetheless, the street was still filthy as hell. That was probably because it was where the garbage trucks came from and not where they went to. I thought about this almost halfway through my second cup of coffee, but I wasn't a city planner and I wasn't a philosopher and I didn't really give a damn anyway. Fortunately, I didn't have to put on a conservative tie and a three-piece suit and drink a little Brim with a mean-minded, vacuous wife and head out for the gray, spirit-grinding office. All I had to do was get dressed and feed the cat. Not a bad life.

I got dressed and fed the cat.

I sat down at my desk and tried to decide what to do next. It was still only ten o'clock in the morning. Whether that was early or late depended on how you looked at it, and I preferred not to. I put my feet up on the desk, smoked my cigar, and winked at the cat, who had now joined me and was sitting about equidistant between the two red telephones that I always kept on my desk at stage left and stage right of my brain. They were both attached to the same line, and when they rang it seemed to enhance the importance of my calls.

The phones rang that Friday morning at 10.17 a.m. I know the precise time because of my custom of logging all incoming calls on my digital computer alarm clock that I keep on my desk. There was nothing alarming about it except for the cat, who was directly in the line of fire and jumped over the moon, the cow, and the fiddle, and my Statue of Liberty thermometer, which read forty-six degrees

Fahrenheit inside the loft. The landlord was really on the ball. Great guy. Probably in Florida.

I picked up the blower and watched the cat settle into a hunkering-down position beside the coffee percolator. She was smarter than some people I knew.

'Hey, man, I was just going through the mail on my desk this morning and there's something here I think you ought to see.' It was Cleve, and whatever it was I didn't want to see it.

'I saw enough last night, pal,' I said.

'Come over here, man. Do it for ol' Cleve.'

'Hang ol' Cleve from the green apple tree.'

I was already in this thing up to my uvula, but if there was a way to get out of it I was sure as hell going to take it. One way was to stay away from the Lone Star. Draw a bye on the Five-Alarm Chili for a while. Country music these days had lost whatever appeal it had had for me. It was hard to believe I'd once been in the thick of it. I was now thinking more along the lines of working on a score for a Broadway musical. Something with class, dignity, intelligence. No steel guitars.

'Don't let me down, man,' said Cleve with a whine in his voice like a blue-ball trucker topping a hill. 'Just come over here one last time . . . All right. If you won't come over here, I'll bring the damn thing over to you now.'

While I waited for Cleve, I paced restlessly back and forth in the kitchen of the loft wishing I were as extinct as the saber-toothed tiger. I just didn't like this business. Give me a nice clean sordid affair to pry into. Murder cases could be hazardous to your health. And it was bad to be cracking heads with Fox and Cooperman before the stiff had even cooled to room temperature. Very bad.

I went to the door and let Cleve in and listened to his grumbling for a while, and then he took a large manila

11

envelope out of his briefcase and placed it on the desk in front of me. It was addressed to Mr Larry Barkin, c/o The Lone Star Cafe, 61 Fifth Avenue, New York, New York.

'Note the date,' said Cleve. 'It was sent last Monday. It arrived in our office on Wednesday, the day before Barkin played the Lone Star. We just assumed it was fan mail, and I hadn't really looked at it until this morning.'

Cleve pushed the envelope closer to me and I noticed his hands were trembling slightly. 'What the hell is in it?' I asked. 'Hate mail? IRS? Greetings from his long-lost ex-wife?'

'Better than that,' said Cleve quietly. 'Why don't you open it and see for yourself?'

I opened the envelope and extracted a colorful piece of sheet music. It was the old Hank Williams song, 'Hey, Good Lookin'.' Cleve looked over my shoulder and together we read the lyrics:

> Hey, hey good lookin', what cha got cookin'
> How's about cookin' somethin' up with me.
> Hey, sweet baby, don't you think maybe
> We could find us a brand new recipe
> I got a hot rod Ford and a two-dollar bill
> And I know a spot right over the hill . . .

There was a sudden chill in the loft, and I felt pretty sure that it had nothing at all to do with wintertime in New York.

5

Cleve had taken his leave. I was taking a little power nap and trying not to dream. I was doing all right. I had succeeded in turning my mind into a small-town drive-in movie screen during the off-season. New York did not exist.

12

It had been there for only a second, like a vaguely familiar bag lady passing quickly by the window of your cab in the rain.

The telephone by the bed seemed to be ringing, so I picked it up.

'Start talkin',' I said in a deep sandpaper voice that would've made Kenny Rogers sound like a castrato. I was in a fairly vicious mood. It was a case of power napus interruptus. I looked outside and it was damn near dark. Then a rather rodentlike voice started yapping at me from the phone. It was Ratso.

Ratso was flea-market flamboyant. New York, New York. He was loyal, intelligent, and thrifty enough to make Scrooge McDuck jealous. He was the editor of *National Lampoon*. Ratso had been right there with me on the first few cases I'd worked on, and I'd almost come to think of him, in my weaker moments, as my American Dr Watson. What went on in Ratso's mind I would not like to hazard a guess, but I liked him so I always gave him a little extra rope. Figured he'd either hang himself or start up a rope factory.

'Hey, man, how you doin'?' said Ratso.

'Could've been worse,' I said. 'Could be snortin' Tide and drinkin' Aqua Velva.'

'Yeah, well, did you see the papers today? You read what happened to Larry Barkin at the Lone Star last night?'

'I didn't need to read the papers, pal. I caught all the action live last night. Or rather dead last night.' I filled Ratso in on the Hank Williams song and the two-dollar bill that I found on Barkin.

'Shit,' said Ratso. 'I must've come too early.'

'Yeah,' I said, 'that's what Uptown Judy told me last night.'

'Seriously, man, I can't believe somebody killed the guy.

13

I saw the whole first set myself and the guy was great. So vibrant. So alive.'

'Yeah, well he was a little stiff by the second set. Look, Ratso, did you notice any strange people hanging around the Lone Star last night during the first show?'

'You kiddin', man?' said Ratso. 'This is New York.'

'I know what it is,' I said. 'I still think you can help me. Maybe it was somebody who didn't look strange.'

'That helps a lot,' said Ratso.

'Look, meet me at the Monkey's Paw in an hour. Is that okay?'

'That's fine,' said Ratso. 'I just hope I can pick you out in the crowd.'

'Bring your bird book and binoculars,' I said and hung up. I walked over to the window and looked down at a dim and nearly deserted Vandam Street. Even the garbage trucks were gone. Tucked away in their little garage-apartments dreaming of coffee grinds and old typewriters somebody'd left out in the snow.

Friday night was the night most people thought they were supposed to have fun. Trouble was most people didn't know what fun was or how to have it, so things usually ended up pretty ugly.

Maybe Daddy'd taken everybody's T-bird away and they just didn't know it yet.

I put on my hat and coat, grabbed a few cigars for the road, and told the cat she was in charge while I was gone. Then I locked the door to the loft, legged it down four flights of stairs, and headed left on Vandam past Hudson to Seventh Avenue. It had gotten colder, if that was possible. The place looked like an excited penguin colony. Everybody was in a hurry but the winos. Newspapers were swirling around all over the sidewalks like somebody's old love letters to yesterday's world.

I smoked a cigar as I walked toward Sheridan Square and the Monkey's Paw, with my hands in my pockets to keep them at least lukewarm. If the Monkey's Paw had been a few blocks farther away I was going to need somebody to help me melt my cold, cold heart.

I thought very briefly about what the back of Larry Barkin's head had looked like the night before. Sort of like some half-rotten, hybrid garden vegetable. I found myself humming 'Hey, Good-Lookin'' as I crossed Seventh Avenue, but it seemed inappropriate so I forced myself to put a sock on it.

The Monkey's Paw was just across Seventh on Bedford Street, one of the few heterosexual bars in the area. It had always had pretensions about being a literary bar. I wasn't so sure of that. It was so cold that heterosexual was good enough for me.

Ratso was standing at the bar. He was wearing green leather pants and a red sweater with little hockey players weaving and checking all over it.

'Hi, Sherlock,' he said.

6

The waitress pointed us to a table about the size of a skateboard. It had a nice view of the garbage cans piled up right outside on Bedford Street.

'Great table,' Ratso said to the waitress.

'Yeah,' I said, 'it looks like the Last Supper table for Jesus and the Seven Dwarfs.'

'Sorry,' said the waitress cheerfully. She was about the sorriest thing I'd seen on ten toes.

The Monkey's Paw was always crowded with tourists on weekends. Intrepid travelers from distant lands like New Jersey. Young couples all the way from the Upper East Side.

Like most Village residents I instinctively disliked these people. Half of them thought they were here for a big night in the city, and the other half thought they were slumming. I didn't like either half, but it doesn't cost anything to be nice.

'You want to move your chair, pal?' I asked a guy who was flapping his mustache to some broad about 'what a dreadful season we're experiencing on Broadway' and blocking my way at the same time.

'Certainly,' he sniffed.

'Yep,' said Ratso in a loud voice as the waitress seated the two of us at the little table ridiculously close to the guy, 'looks like the theater's really dead.'

'Modulate your voice, will you,' I said to Ratso. 'This guy gets hostile and he'll beat us both to death with his cookie duster.'

Ratso ordered a vodka and soda and I ordered a Prior Dark with a shot of Old Grand-Dad to keep it company. The table was starting to get a little crowded, but if you live in New York you don't go out looking for elbow room. You just try to get your shot glass from your hand to your mouth. Sometimes it's harder than it looks.

'Hey,' I said, 'that's McGovern's drink you ordered.' McGovern was half Irish and half Indian and worked on the national desk of the *Daily News*. He'd been eighty-sixed from the Monkey's Paw years ago for urinating on the leg of a patron.

Ratso smiled. 'As long as it's not Elijah's drink,' he said. Who Elijah was was hard to explain, except that I doubted if he worked for the *Daily News*.

'You know,' said Ratso, 'they say the lady that McGovern peed on has never been back here.'

'Neither has McGovern,' I said.

'Neither has Elijah,' said Ratso.

'I'll drink to that,' I said and we ordered another round. Things had cleared a little by now. The theater crowd, so to speak, had left, and I eased my chair back a little.

'This was Dylan Thomas's drink, you know. Drank eighteen straight shots of Old Grand-Dad down at the White Horse Tavern before he fell through the trapdoor into the downstairs bedroom.'

'Okay,' said Ratso, dismissing the subject, 'how can I help?'

'You can stop me at seventeen,' I said. I signaled the waitress for another shot. Ratso nursed his drink.

'You were there,' I said, 'in Larry Barkin's dressing room.' Ratso nodded. 'What did you see? Who did you see?' I had a pretty good idea from Cleve what the list of suspects looked like, but I wanted to hear it again from Ratso.

'Cast your mind back,' I encouraged him.

'Certainly, Monsieur Poirot,' he said. 'There was a blond. A photographer. Her name was Gunner.'

'That's a funny name,' I said.

'So's Kinky,' said Ratso.

'Go on,' I said.

'There was a bald-headed lawyer passing out cocaine to everybody – '

'That description could fit just about everyone I know.'

'Now listen to this,' said Ratso. 'Your old pal Chet Flippo was there. Very chummy with Barkin. Very chummy. And of course your rapierlike memory bank will recall the title of Chet's latest book . . .'

Chet was an old friend of mine from Texas who had written a book recently that had turned Nashville and country music lovers in general into at least three armed camps. One group loved it. One group hated it. One group thought it was a little ho-hum. I hadn't read the book yet

17

myself but I knew the title: *Your Cheatin' Heart: A Biography of Hank Williams.*

'A bit obvious, wouldn't you think?'

'I'm just tellin' you who was there, Sherlock. You put it in your pipe and smoke it.' I lit a cigar.

'There was also your friend Mike Simmons. He was playing Barkin's guitar, I think, trying to show him a song or something.'

'I'll bet he was,' I said. Simmons was one of the best country singers I'd ever heard, but he would take a drink. He was crazy, talented, and frustrated. Like everybody else in New York.

'Simmons was pretty bombed all right,' said Ratso. 'I was kind of worried he was going to break Barkin's guitar.'

'Yeah,' I said. I puffed on the cigar thoughtfully. I killed the shot and ordered another one. Ratso ordered another vodka and soda.

'Okay,' I said, when the drinks arrived, 'what've we got?'

'We've got,' said Ratso, 'the blond photographer, the bald-headed lawyer who was dispensing cocaine, Chet Flippo, and Mike Simmons.'

'What about Bill Dick?' I asked.

'Bill Dick owns the club,' said Ratso.

'My dear Ratso,' I said, 'I've worked with a great many club owners, and I've found that they're capable of anything.'

'Well, then,' said Ratso, 'we've got five suspects. It looks pretty easy.'

'Right,' I killed the shot and signaled the waitress to drop the hatchet.

'You're stopping at five Old Grand-Dads?' asked Ratso. 'I'm quite disillusioned.'

'I'm sure you are,' I said as I paid the check and watched

Ratso pretend to look for his money. 'What's the matter, pal, you got fishhooks in your pockets?'

We walked outside.

'Well, thanks for a lovely evening,' said Ratso. 'I'm going home to spank my monkey.'

'Fine,' I said. 'Let's keep in touch on this thing. It could turn fairly ugly.'

As I walked home in the cold I thought the whole business over. Getting into a murder investigation was a little like getting into drugs or alcohol.

As my old friend Slim used to say back in Texas, 'sometimes you gotta find what you like and let it kill you.'

7

Early Saturday morning I was sawing away on a particularly peaceful Perma-Log when the phones rang. The voice came over the wire like a chain saw that had cut its teeth in Brooklyn.

'We can't have it. We just can't have it. Right or wrong, Kinkster?'

'Right, Bill,' I said sleepily. It was Bill Dick, the owner of the Lone Star. He might've had a weak last name but he had a strong set of lungs. Maybe it was the hour.

I sat up in bed and looked first at the cat and then at the clock. The cat yawned. The clock said nine-thirty.

'What can't we have, Bill?' I asked. I eyed the coffee percolator in the kitchen like a long-lost lover.

'We can't have a maniac running loose around the Lone Star,' he said.

'Where were you Thursday night, Bill?' I asked a bit too abruptly.

'I was sailing, for Christ's sake. Out in the goddamn boat. Got back last night. Never thought anything like this could

19

happen. I like to sail. Get away from the rat race. Man's got a nice boat. Man likes to sail. Can't work all the time. Right or wrong, Kinkster?'

'Right, Bill,' I said.

'Look,' he said, 'you helped make the Lone Star what it is, Kinkster. You performed here many times and you profited from those performances. The cops have been here. Been here several times. But they're lost at sea without a sail. Will you take the wheel, Kinkster? Will you find who murdered Larry Barkin? Will you do it for the Lone Star?'

'Well, Jesus, Bill,' I said, 'since you put it that way. I guess I'll do it for God and country music.'

'That's the spirit,' said Bill Dick. 'We'll get to the bottom of this. Right or wrong, Kinkster?'

'Right, Bill,' I said. I hung up. I put some coffee in the percolator along with a bit of old eggshell for flavor, and while I waited for it to perk I fired up a cigar.

'Home is the sailor,' I said to the cat. 'Home from the sea.' I gave her some tuna for breakfast.

I didn't figure I owed God much. And I didn't think I owed country music the time of day. I didn't even owe anything to the Lone Star except maybe an old bar bill from way back when. About all I owed was what I owed to McGovern, fifty dollars, and since he would no doubt put the fifty dollars to ill use, I was really doing him a favor by not paying him for a while. Not that I didn't have the assets.

I was on my second cup of coffee and slightly past the midway point of the cigar I'd lit after I'd talked to Bill Dick. I didn't usually like to smoke a cigar past the midway point. I liked to store them for a while in the wastebasket and fire up the remaining portion at a later date. In the manner of a fine wine, you had to let a half-smoked cigar

20

age a bit. Had to let it breathe. A lot of people didn't understand this, but I didn't understand a lot of people.

I smoke as many as ten cigars a day and I expect to live forever. Of course I don't inhale. I just blow the smoke at small children, green plants, vegetarians, and anybody who happens to be jogging by at the same time that I'm exhaling.

You have to work at it if you want to be a good smoker. Especially today with all the nonsmoking world constantly harassing you. It's enough to make you drink. I poured a shot of Jameson Irish Whiskey into a third cup of coffee and I sat down at my desk.

I thought of what Charles Lamb, the renowned British essayist, had said when someone asked him how he could smoke so many cigars and pipes. He said: 'I toil after it, sir, as some men toil after virtue.' Not bad, Chuck.

I placed a call to Sergeant Cooperman at the Sixth Precinct but he was out protecting the public. The desk sergeant said he'd get back to me. I called Mike Simmons.

'Hey, Mike,' I said, 'how about a little liquor drink for the heat?'

'The heat is right,' said Simmons. 'This Sergeant Cooperman character's been covering my ass like an Indian blanket.'

'That's hardly the way to speak of New York's finest, Simmons,' I reminded him.

'Where?' he asked.

'Where what?'

'The liquor drink for the heat.'

'City Limits. Ten o'clock.'

'See you there,' he said.

I decided to take a little power nap, but when I woke up it was almost eight o'clock. As luck would have it, I didn't dream. Or if I had dreamed, I didn't remember anything, which is almost as good. I jumped into the rain-room and took a shower. Sang a little Hank Williams medley. 'Cold, Cold Heart,' 'Your Cheatin' Heart,' – Hank apparently had had a thing about hearts – and 'I'll Never Get Out of This World Alive.' The lyrics to the chorus of the last song went:

> 'No matter how I struggle and strive
> I'll never get out of this world alive.'

That seemed like a good place to stop. I dried off with a towel I had inadvertently taken from the Chelsea Hotel. It said YMCA on it.

They say Dylan Thomas died while he was staying at the Chelsea. Many places claim Homer's birth and many places claim Dylan Thomas' death. What does that tell us? Nothing, I thought. I decided against shaving. Go for the Yessir You're-a-fart Look. Very in these days.

I spread the towel out on the cold, cold radiator to either dry or mildew as the case might be. John Lennon, Nina Simone, Abbie Hoffman, and Sid Vicious had also stayed at the Chelsea, and so had the guy who wrote the song 'Tubby the Tuba.' Quite a clientele.

I got dressed, threw on my old hunting vest, left the cat in charge, and split. I headed up Hudson and then snaked over toward Seventh Avenue. On Grove Street there was a young woman sitting on a wooden chair on the sidewalk playing a cello. The big cello case was open in front of her. It looked like a coffin for a large child. There were a few quarters and dimes and nickels in it and that was all. Chump change in anybody's league. I stood there in the cold and listened for a moment. She sounded pretty good, but what I knew about the cello you could put in a ukelele case and rattle it around a bit.

On the brick wall above her I noticed a bronze plaque. It was a bust of Thomas Paine, who'd died on this site in 1809 after being tortured on his deathbed by clergymen. On the sides of the plaque, slightly grimy but still readable, were two of Paine's credos: 'The world is my country' and 'To do good is my religion'.

I gave the girl a five-dollar bill. I figured anyone who could play the cello in this weather deserved something. She nodded thanks to me. Kind of world-weary. Kind of sweet.

I headed over to City Limits, a rather funky country music bar in the heart of the Village, to meet Simmons. At Seventh Avenue I turned back to look at the girl, and she was playing the cello as if I were still standing in front of her. Never get to Carnegie Hall, I thought.

'Course, why would you want to go to Carnegie Hall when you could go to the Carnegie Delicatessen?

8

City Limits was the place you went when you'd had all the fun you could take at the Lone Star and it was still only two o'clock in the morning. When it was four o'clock in the morning and you'd had all the fun you could possibly stand at City Limits, you'd put your brain in a wheelchair and navigate over to the Zodiac, an after-hours bar that resembled what all the concentric circles of hell would look like if they were suddenly compressed into one large, dark, loud, rather tedious pancake. After having fun at the Zodiac, you'd walk out into the blinding sunlight and grinding traffic of Canal Street at 9.00 a.m. of a workaday morning and you'd know what it meant to wish you were dead. Fun was hard work in New York.

I nodded to Glen, the bouncer who worked the door at City Limits. Glen was a big guy with a long ponytail that nobody ever pulled except a little old lady from Idaho one night who thought it was her scarf.

'Is Mr Simmons here?' I asked him.

'Not for long,' he said ominously. He waved me in and I put the two bucks cover charge back in my pocket. Fifteen years dying slowly on the road so I could get into dumps like this without paying the cover. Us big celebrities had it made.

Simmons was standing at the bar. He was drinking Jack Daniel's on the rocks.

'Hey, man,' he shouted at me, 'now that you're in the black, I'll buy you a drink.' It appeared as if he'd had a few already.

'Okay,' I said. 'I'll have a Lone Star beer for three dollars and fifty cents.'

'Shit,' he said, 'you can do better than that.'

'All right,' I said, 'give me a Chivas on the rocks with a little splash of New York tap water in it. Cuts the bite.'

'Naw,' said Simmons, 'that's too complicated.'

'Courvoisier,' I said.

'Naw,' said Simmons in a loud voice. 'That's too sophisticated for this goddamn low-life dive.' I looked over my shoulder and saw the large bartender wearing some kind of biker's vest, a cowboy hat, and a scowl.

'Give us a moment, pal,' I said. He turned away in disgust.

'Simmons,' I said, 'this may look like a goddamn low-life dive to you, but actually, what these people are trying to do is re-create the ambience of the early country and western honky-tonk. Also,' I said, 'you might want to modulate your voice or they might try to re-create it on the bridge of your nose.' He laughed.

'Give me a Jameson,' I said.

'Naw,' said Simmons, 'that's too damn ethnic, man. You don't want a Jameson.' I'd made the mistake of giving Simmons a cigar, and he was now gesturing with it and

24

precariously waving the lighted end in front of the eyes of nearby patrons. I turned for a moment and watched the band on the little stage across the room. I recognized a few of the pickers. They were pretty good. They had talent. And talent was its own reward. It had to be. That was about all they were going to get playing three brutal sets for jaded strangers from the Upper West Side and people waiting for the Zodiac to open. But the band was playing and the people were dancing.

I saw that the drummer was a guy who'd played a few concert tours with me in the bleary past. He looked over at me, waved a stick, and shrugged, as if to say 'Help! Get me out of here.' He was a talented drummer. But most landlords I'd known didn't take talent when the rent came due. I needed a drink.

'Simmons,' I said, 'order me a drink or I'll kill you.'

'Barkeep,' Simmons shouted, 'two double Black Jacks. Rocks. Walking now, make 'em fly.'

The bartender, in a slow and surly fashion, brought two double Jack Daniel's over to us. Simmons was having trouble holding his glass, but he raised it now rather precariously in a toast. He clinked the bottom of it against the top of mine and said, 'Never above you.' Then he clinked the top of it against the bottom of mine. 'Never below you,' he said. Then he put his arm around my shoulder and slammed his glass dangerously against my glass and said, 'Always by your side.'

'Don't link our karma, pal,' I said.

We both took a slug of the Jack.

I disengaged my shoulder from Simmons' arm and walked a little closer to the bandstand. The guitar player had reversed the strings on his guitar and was playing it left-handed. It wasn't unheard of. I'd seen it before. But it did make me think of something that had been nagging

25

at me since I'd visited the late Larry Barkin in his dressing room at the Lone Star. I picked up a handful of peanuts from a barrel in the middle of the floor and walked back over to Simmons at the bar.

'Mike,' I said, 'you wouldn't be a southpaw, would you?'

'Who wants to know?' he said belligerently.

'Who the hell do you think wants to know?' I asked. 'Who do you see standing here talking to you?'

'I see Spade Cooley,' he said. Spade Cooley was a country singer who stomped his wife to death, served time in prison, and passed on painfully to hillbilly heaven.

The band had taken a break, and I went over and talked with them for a while. When I looked over at the bar for Simmons, I could see an altercation taking place. Simmons was struggling with a well-dressed woman. The big bartender had him around the neck, and Glen the bouncer was hurrying over in the direction of the trouble.

They wouldn't hurt Simmons inside the bar but I'd seen some of City Limit's Neanderthals work over rowdy patrons in the alley down the street from the club. I figured I'd meet them right outside the door and take Simmons off their big, remorseless, country music hands. Not that he didn't deserve it.

I stood out on Tenth Street in the cold and waited. The door to the place burst open and Simmons came flying out onto the sidewalk. Shaking with rage, he picked himself up and started back toward the club. I grabbed his arm but he managed to pry the door open, and with me holding on to him, he staggered a few steps back into the place. Glen and his ponytail started toward us, then stopped. Simmons roared over the noise and din of the bar.

'You'd throw Hank fucking Williams out of here!' he said.

26

9

I put Simmons in a cab and told the driver to take him to Marylou's on Ninth Street, where the atmosphere was friendlier. He would not go home, and I knew there was no way to make him. Home was a meaningless word in New York. Sometimes it was nowhere. Apparently it meant little to Simmons. Except for the fact that the cat was there, it didn't mean a hell of a lot to me either.

I had learned nothing from Simmons except that I shouldn't go back to City Limits with him again. I didn't even learn if he was left-handed.

I went to a pay phone across the street from Village Cigars and called Chet Flippo at The Writers' Room on Waverly. It was a quiet place he sometimes went to work on his current projects and to hide from the noise and disruption that was New York. I wondered if there could be anything else he was hiding from.

I had only five suspects to work on at the moment, though I might be narrowing or enlarging the field once I knew more. Ratso and Cleve were probably out of it. Ratso made a fairly adequate modern-day Watson and I couldn't really afford to lose him, and Cleve had been the one who'd gotten me involved in the Barkin affair to begin with. Bill Dick had been on his goddamn boat. Chet Flippo and Mike Simmons were both friends of mine, but when I thought about it, that didn't really put them in the clear. Where murder was concerned, you had to be a little more analytical about people than you would if you were merely sending out Bar Mitzvah invitations.

Then there was the bald-headed, cocaine-dispensing lawyer and the lovely limey shutterbug. Couldn't overlook them. But I was already getting an ugly feeling about this case.

I bought a couple of nice ropes at Village Cigars and walked briskly across Sheridan Square. In this weather you had to walk briskly. If you didn't, you might freeze, and some avant-garde SoHo artist might try to mount you in his gallery as an ice sculpture. You had to be careful crossing Sheridan Square in any season. Somebody might try just to mount you.

The High Five was a step down from the street and from a lot of other places, too. It was a jazz-oriented bar that took 'seedy' to a whole other level. The High Five had a liberal sprinkling of interracial couples around for local color. Most of them appeared to be heterosexual, but you couldn't have everything. One of the nice things about the joint was that no matter who the hell you were, you never looked out of place.

Flippo was sitting at the bar when I got there. He looked at me with colorless eyes through steel-rimmed glasses. He did not look happy. 'Sit down,' he said.

I hadn't seen Chet Flippo in a long time. When I thought about it, maybe I'd never seen Chet Flippo. 'Have a drink,' he said. He looked harmless enough, but I'd been on the circuit long enough to know that harmless enough was always dangerous. Since 1982 I hadn't even trusted the Easter Bunny.

I ordered a shot of Irish whiskey and a Bass ale to keep it company on the mahogany. 'Used to be a nice place,' I said. 'Charlie Parker and Edith Piaf used to hang out here.' Flippo looked around a little at the squalor with disbelief in his eyes.

'That's what they say,' I said. He sipped his draft beer nervously. 'Cops talk to you, Chester?' I asked.

'Affirmative,' he said, nodding his head sharply once.

'What'd they want to know? They ask you about your old parking tickets?'

28

'I told them I didn't drive,' he said.

'Quite sensible,' I said. Even A. J. Foyt took a hack in the city. 'Okay, Chester,' I said, 'what happened Thursday night in Barkin's dressing room? Spit it, pal.' I killed the shot and looked right at him.

'Barkin and I've known each other on and off for a long time,' said Flippo. 'I've reviewed a few of his shows for various magazines. I never liked his sugar-coated music and he never liked my acid-toned journalistic style, but we both had a grudging professional respect for each other's work.'

'Okay,' I said, 'spare me everybody's résumé. Nutshell the damn thing.'

'Well, I'd been up there a little while talking with Barkin. Maybe fifteen minutes. That photographer, I believe her name was Gunner something or other, she was there the whole time, snapping away. The bartender, Cleve, and the bouncer, they all came in and out at various times while I was there. This was after the first set. Pretty good show, actually.'

'Glad you enjoyed it. Pray continue,' I said irritably, as I ordered another shot.

'Your friend Ratso had managed to worm his way in there. I think Barkin wanted him out of the dressing room for some reason.'

'Quite understandable,' I said.

'Ratso was still there when I left the first time to go to the cloakroom and get a copy of the book for Barkin.'

'The book?' I asked.

'My book on Hank Williams. I gave a copy to Barkin.'

'Curious,' I said.

'Not really,' said Flippo. 'I give copies to any number of – '

'That's not what I meant, pal. You missed the harbor on that one. I meant it was curious because the book was gone

29

when I got there. The body was there but the book was gone.'

'Yeah, well, I autographed one for him and brought it back up to him. They'd gotten rid of Ratso by then. And that's about it.'

'You didn't notice a bald-headed lawyer distributing cocaine to everybody?' I asked.

'No, I didn't,' said Flippo. 'I've got a fine eye for detail. I would've noticed something like that.' He chuckled to himself, but the chuckle didn't quite reach his eyes. They were still colorless, emotionless through the steel-rimmed glasses, like a Nazi villain's in a late-night movie.

'Excuse me,' I said. 'I'm going to hit the ladies' room.' He raised an eyebrow but I let it pass. I walked to the back of the place to a tiny hallway where the bathrooms and the pay phone were. The men's room at the High Five I knew from experience was invariably in such a state of extreme disarray so as to make it highly unsuitable for even casual usage. It went way beyond 'out of order.' You wouldn't want to straighten your bow tie in the place.

One deal had apparently just transpired in the ladies' room because when I walked in, three very cool, noncommittal guys walked out. Didn't even nod at me.

I didn't linger very long, but it was long enough to notice that somebody had whizzed in the sink. That in itself was nothing new. People had been doing that since Lenny Bruce became the first modern man to piss in a sink and to attach a certain amount of importance to it. Doubtless somebody in some primitive Australopithecine culture had probably pissed in a sink before Bruce. But could you call it a sink? And could you call it culture?

By the time I got back to Chet Flippo at the bar, he'd already paid the bill and was taking a copy of his book out of a briefcase on the floor. The bartender picked up the money from the bar, and as he counted it I thought I saw a two-dollar bill flash by between a sawbuck and a single. I didn't say anything.

Flippo autographed the book and handed it to me. He'd signed his autograph left-handed. As we walked out, I looked at the cover. It read: *Your Cheatin' Heart: A Biography of Hank Williams.*

'Catchy title,' I said.

10

Sunday was the Lord's day. He could have it. Sundays were lonely, family-oriented, and fairly unproductive in the investigation of murder. Most people went to church on Sunday. Even Bill Dick, who belonged to the Church of the Latter-Day Businessman, probably went to church on Sunday. If he wasn't out on his goddamn boat. Afterward, most people would do Sunday kinds of things like jog, go for a picnic in the park, or drive their cars slowly.

Of course, you didn't see too many picknickers in New York. The parks in the area were not real conducive to picnics. Also, the weather was as cold as Chet Flippo's eyes.

But the good thing about Sundays that almost made up for all the other crap was the total, unearthly absence of garbage trucks. You could grind your teeth in peace. You could really get into a hangover. You could cling to the tattered fabric of your dreams.

Sunday was also a great day for reflections. I looked in the mirror. Decided not to shave.

I made some coffee. I fed the cat. I took a kitchen match and lit a two-dollar and twenty-five-cent Partagas cigar. Always keeping it well above the flame. I paced around the loft in my purple bathrobe.

I made a little bet with myself. Who would call first,

Uptown Judy or Downtown Judy? The smart money was probably on Downtown Judy. She was possibly a little lonelier and a little unhappier at this time in her life, but who knew? Christ, I thought, maybe I'll call one of them.

The time seemed right to conduct a small Sherlockian experiment I'd been thinking about since I'd seen the left-handed guitar player at City Limits. I got my guitar case out of the closet, knocked off a few cobwebs, and opened it up. My guitar was an Ovation, the kind with the big, rounded back to it that, when you played it, always made you look fatter than you were. It had a wide fingerboard, about the same size as the one on Larry Barkin's Gibson.

The experiment I was attempting was not a strictly scientific one, but I hoped it would shed some light on the gloom of what I was pleased to call the investigation. I leaned the guitar against my desk and walked purposefully into the kitchen. I took the little black puppet head from its place on top of the refrigerator near the kitchen window. I placed it squarely in the middle of the kitchen table and walked back to the desk to get the guitar.

The only ways you could kill somebody with a guitar were to hit him with the sides of it or to bash him, mortar and pestle-like, with the fat tail-end of the sound box. One other method commonly used was to bore the victim to death by playing it. Such was not the case here, however. Nor, from the appearance of Barkin's guitar, was the mortar and pestle method employed. The killer I was looking for had used the most common approach to guitar murder – the Mickey Mantle method, in which the guitar is swung like a baseball bat in an effort to take the victim's head downtown. All this, I felt, was clearly indicated. Even the cops knew it.

The point of contact on Barkin's Gibson had been the top side of the sound box. I'd seen that in the dressing room.

Some country singers tape cheat sheets on this part of their ax, with song titles, jokes, and maybe the name of the town they're in if they've been on the road for a long time. I never taped cheat sheets to my guitar. Always used the inside of my hat.

I took a few trial swings at the puppet head from the left-hand side. I held the guitar with both hands around the fingerboard. I held it close to the neck. Faceup. That was the way Barkin's attacker had probably done it. The guitar felt comfortable in my hands. I took a whack at the puppet head just for the hell of it, swinging from left to right. Sent it flying across the room. The cat jumped onto the desk. The cat detested violence of any sort.

'Relax,' I said. 'This is just a test.' I retrieved the puppet head and put it back on the table. Now came the crucial part of the experiment. I turned the guitar facedown and took a few trial swings from the right-hand side. The fingerboard felt awkward, nearly slipping from my grasp. The steel strings cut into my fingers. It was almost a chore to hold the guitar level because of the rounded shape of the guitar neck. It would be exceedingly difficult, I thought, to take a solid swing from the right side with the guitar in a facedown position. In other words, if a righty had croaked Barkin, he would have held the guitar faceup. But then the guitar would have been smashed on the bottom part of the sound box. The guitar was damaged on the top part of the sound box. Therefore, unless I'd missed my guess badly, Barkin's murderer was left-handed.

I went directly to the phone and dialed Mike Simmons' number. It was 3.17 p.m. but I woke him from a dead slumber on the fourth ring.

'Mike,' I said with some urgency, 'leap sideways.'

'Huh?' he said.

'Mike,' I said. 'This is Kinky. Look, are you left-handed?'

'Yeah,' he said, with some little irritation. 'Why?'

'No problem,' I said. 'It's nothing.'

'Then why the fuck did you wake me up and ask me if I'm left-handed?' It was a logical question, and I hadn't been wholly unprepared for it. But I still had to think on my feet. I took a healthy puff of the cigar I was smoking.

'We're having a Lefty Frizzell look-alike contest, Simmons,' I said, 'and I wanted to be sure you qualified.' I hung up the phone.

Lefty Frizzell was a great country singer who died a number of years ago. But he still worked fine in a pinch.

I dialed the number of the Lone Star Cafe. I heard the sound of music and laughter in the background. Business might be down because of Larry Barkin's murder, but the Lone Star seemed to be doing the best with what it had. Probably take a hydrogen bomb to put a sock on the place.

'Lone Star Cafe,' came a sweet, insipid voice.

'Yeah,' I said, 'is Cleve there?'

'Who's calling, please?' she asked.

'Tell him it's Kinky,' I said.

'Oh, Kinky,' the voice gushed, 'when are you going to play the Lone Star again?'

'Not for a while,' I said, 'under the circumstances.'

'Oh,' she said. 'Just a moment.' Saccharine, recorded country music came on the line while I waited. Sounded like a Larry Barkin song. Then Cleve picked up the phone.

'Cleve,' I said, ' can you help me with something?'

'This ain't Opportunity Hot Line, but I'll see what I can do,' he said.

'That's the spirit,' I said. 'What's that British bird's name, luv, and will you give me the number of her telly?'

'You want the number of her television set?' Cleve asked.

'No, goddammit,' I said. 'Give me the number of what-

34

ever they call their telephones.' He gave me Gunner's full name and phone number.

'She left-handed?' I asked.

'Beg pardon?'

'You heard me,' I said. 'Is she left-handed?' It didn't take me long to get short with Cleve.

'Wouldn't know,' he said.

'I'll find out,' I said. Even if she was right-handed, it didn't necessarily put her in the clear. She might have had an accomplice who bashed Barkin. Maybe she only garroted him with his little pink cowboy tie. But that was unlikely. In fact, the whole damn thing was unlikely.

'What about the bald-headed lawyer who dispenses cocaine?'

'What about him?' asked Cleve.

'Is he left-handed?'

'I don't even know who he is,' said Cleve. 'But he does offer you the coke straw with his right hand.'

'Inconclusive,' I murmured. I thanked Cleve and cradled the blower. Either I had a lot of work to do or I didn't have a damn thing to do. I didn't know enough about the case to know which.

I walked over to the kitchen and found a bottle of Jameson and my old bull's horn shot glass and took them both back with me over to the desk. I poured a fairly liberal amount into the bull's horn. I had made the polite gesture of a toast to the cat and had managed to manipulate the bull's horn almost to my lips when the phone rang.

Delicately balancing the bull's horn, I reached for the blower on the left. 'Start talkin,' I said rather curtly.

'Hi, honey,' said the voice on the phone. 'What's going on? What did you do today? I missed you.'

It was Downtown Judy. I downed the shot.

11

The next few days went by in what some are wont to call a mindless blur. Actually, that wasn't quite accurate. Some of the tedium was pretty well defined. Like my meeting Tuesday afternoon with Bill Dick at the Lone Star Cafe. Cleve sat in on the meeting. We had a three-Lone Star beer lunch.

'Jesus Christ,' said Bill Dick, 'these bozos are only on the road three hundred ninety-seven days a year. You'd think they might find some other place to get themselves bumped off. Maybe Nashville or Austin or someplace. They've got country music down there, don't they?'

'Yeah,' I said. 'It's probably better, too.' Dick glared at me.

'Well, maybe not Nashville,' I said.

The bartender brought us three bowls of Five-Alarm Chili and another round of beer.

Dick hoisted his bottle of Lone Star in the air and looked me right in the eye. 'No matter how successful I get,' he said, 'no matter if I own this place or what, I still drink my beer from the bottle. That's the kind of guy I am. Right or wrong, Kinkster?'

'Right, Bill,' I said. I took another drink from my glass.

'I'm not a phony. I never bullshit you. Right or wrong, Kinkster?'

'Right, Bill,' I said.

'And I'm worried. I'm real worried. If we don't catch this killer, we can bring down the big top . . . drop the curtain . . . set our horses free . . . cut the mainsail . . .'

He took a drink from his bottle and mixed another metaphor or two. Then he was through. I looked on silently and stirred my chili.

If the meeting at the Lone Star hadn't been a raging success,

I was having even more trouble getting in touch with Princess Di. Maybe the British photographer broad was hiding in her darkroom trying to develop her alibi. I'd left five messages on her machine in the past three days and I was running out of charm. I was also running out of cat food. All I had left was one can of sliced veal in gravy. The cat hated sliced veal in gravy. I'd found her one wintry night back when she was just a little kitten lost in an alley in Chinatown. If she had made it across Canal Street into Little Italy, she probably would have liked sliced veal in gravy.

I figured I'd give my British bird call one more try, and if that didn't work I'd probably have to go on a field trip. It was 6.07 of a Wednesday evening by the computer clock when I finally connected with Gunner.

'Hello,' she said very briskly. Sounded like she was in a hurry to set up a tripod. Like she had to rush to catch something before it went away. I was used to that. All photographers sounded that way. Except the ones who worked for the morgue.

'Sixth time's a charm, eh what?' I said.

'Who is this?' she asked. I wasn't Professor Higgins, but her accent sounded good to me.

'F. Stop Fitzgerald,' I said. Thought I'd try a lighthearted approach.

'Who the bloody hell is this?' she stormed. An accent, like so many other components of a woman, is really more attractive when the woman is a little angry. You shouldn't point it out though, unless you want the woman to get really angry, which is never attractive.

'Look,' I said, 'my name is Kinky. I got your number from Cleve at the Lone Star. I'm doing some work for them on this Barkin situation. I need to talk to you.'

'The police have already spoken to me.'

'I know that. I still want to talk to you.'

37

'You're not a detective, are you?' she asked.

'I'm not from the Yard,' I said, 'but I am a close friend of Mick Brennan's.' Mick was a celebrated British freelancer, who had, among other exploits, covered the Argentine mainland during the Falklands War and lived to tell about it, which he often did. Brennan was also a friend of Michael Caine's, for what it was worth.

'You know Mick Brennan?' she asked. She was interested now. Probably saw a good career move.

'Sure, I know Mick,' I said. 'Saw him a few weeks ago. Tavern on the Green, I think it was.' Men's room at the Monkey's Paw was actually where I'd seen Brennan, but far be it from me to destroy a young girl's illusion. One tavern's as good as another.

'Kinky,' she said, 'a man has been murdered. I don't give a damn about Mick Brennan or about you. If I talk to you it will be because I feel a moral responsibility to help apprehend a vicious, brutal, cold-blooded killer, not because of who you are or who you know.'

'Sounds like fun,' I said.

'We may as well get this over with now,' she said with a rather British-sounding sigh. 'Do you know where I live?'

She gave me the address.

Ten minutes later I was hacking it up Third Avenue to Thirty-eighth Street.

Another ten minutes and the doorman at Gunner's building was giving me the old fish eye and calling up to see if I was who I said I was. Or at least if who I said I was was who she was expecting. It was and I was. I took the elevator up to the fourth floor.

Gunner came to the door. She was handsome, blond, British, and, it emerged, right-handed. She made some tea while I looked around the living room. It really wasn't a living room at all; it was a photography studio with two teacups in it.

The tea seemed to thaw her out a bit, but she didn't tell me much that I didn't already know. And that wasn't much. She'd already turned over to the cops all the rolls she shot in the Lone Star dressing room. She'd briefly met Chet Flippo, Mike Simmons, Ratso, and, of course, Larry Barkin and his two brothers, both of whom had apparently used a smaller dressing room down the hall. She had shot the pictures of Barkin for a European fashion magazine, which either demonstrated that country music was getting very trendy or that European fashion editors were pretty slow out of the chute. She had seen, but did not meet, the bald-headed lawyer.

Her cat was named Dennis.

'Look, Gunner,' I said, 'I know you don't give a damn about me or Mick Brennan, but why not come join us for a drink at least. I'm on my way to meet him now.'

'Well, Kinky . . . ,' she said. It was a coy, hearty, sort of well-bred come-on, and I liked the inflection she was starting to give to the 'Kinky' part.

We walked up Third Avenue to Forty-fourth Street and halfway down Forty-fourth to Costello's Bar. Costello's was the haunt of practically every newspaperman in New York who would take a drink, and that was practically every newspaperman in New York.

We went in and walked to the far end of the bar. I noticed a fair number of heads turning. The shutterbug wasn't bad in the visual department. I didn't know how bright she was, how devious she could be, or what she was like when she took her camera off, but she did have the strength of character not to give a damn about me or Mick Brennan. And she was making a few waves at Costello's.

Brennan was sitting at the very end of the bar

accompanied by a Heineken and by my old pal McGovern from the *Daily News*. McGovern was working on an extremely large vodka and tonic. Neither glanced up as we came over.

'Here's trouble,' said Brennan. They both looked fairly heavily monstered.

'Gunner,' I said, 'this is my friend McGovern from the *Daily News*.'

'And I'm Jimmy Olsen from the *Daily Planet*,' said Brennan.

'And this is my intrepid young photographer friend, Gunner,' I said. McGovern laughed a loud, almost obscene laugh. Gunner ignored it.

'I admire your work, Mr Brennan,' said Gunner, 'and I've seen your by-line quite often, Mr McGovern.'

'That's more than he can say for himself,' said Brennan.

'Charmed,' said McGovern.

Gunner and I sat down at the bar next to the two of them. She ordered a glass of red wine and I ordered a shot of Jameson with a pint of Victoria bitters. Gunner and Brennan ran a little compulsory photography shoptalk, and I had a chance to ask McGovern for a little favor.

'Can you help me with something, McGovern?' I asked politely.

'No,' said McGovern.

'It's important,' I said.

'Out of the question,' said McGovern. I ordered another round for the four of us.

'I'd like to know what you have in the files on Chet Flippo. He's a music journalist. Has a book out on Hank Williams. I'd like to know what else he's done. Also everything you have on Larry Barkin, the country singer who got himself croaked last week.'

'Call me tomorrow afternoon at the city desk.'

'You're a real pal, McGovern,' I said.

'Don't I know it,' he said.

'Want to see some shots of the creature?' asked Gunner as she reached into the large bag she was carrying.

'I've already shot plenty of McGovern,' said Brennan.

'I mean the creature on top of the Lone Star Cafe,' said Gunner.

'The iguana,' explained McGovern to Brennan. The iguana was a famous fifty-foot-long metal monster that had been created by an artist friend of mine, Bob Wade, from Dallas. It was so hideous-looking that the squeamish Fifth Avenue Merchant Association got the city to order the monster taken down. But by that time the iguana had become so famous as to almost be a tourist attraction, and the city reversed itself and ordered the creature reinstated, to Bob Wade's extreme gratification and the Merchant Association's extreme mortification. Today its huge head glares triumphantly over Fifth Avenue.

All you have to do to get a closer look at the iguana is to wait until the security guy at the club goes down to the men's room. Then you get up to the third floor and worm your way into the dressing room at the end of the hallway. Ask Ratso how it's done. Then pry open the unlocked metal door that leads on to the roof, and you're right there standing about even with the iguana's somewhat unkempt toenails and looking up right into its giant Fifth Avenue-hating eyes. Pleasant spot for a mint julep. Had a few other things there myself, including one of the waitresses at the club.

Gunner took out a contact sheet and a loupe and put them both on the bar. Brennan and McGovern leaned forward to have a look. I took my time about it, having already seen the iguana almost every time I'd played the Lone Star and also in some of my milder nightmares.

'When did you take these?' I asked Gunner.

'Last Thursday night,' said Gunner. 'The roll's just of the iguana and a few shots of some men playing chess in Washington Square Park, so I didn't bother to develop it until this morning. The police wanted everything else I shot that night.'

I leaned forward toward the contact sheet with only a lukewarm interest. I didn't see it at first. I picked up the loupe and gave a cursory glance at several frames. Near the middle of the sheet I stopped the loupe. I'd almost missed it.

When I backtracked with the loupe one frame, it hit me like a haymaker from Joe Palooka. The door that led out to the roof was open, and on a distant wall of the dressing-room was what appeared to be a blurry shadow.

'What do you make of it, Mick?' I asked Brennan.

'It's a picture of a man making a hand shadow of a duck, mate,' he said. I heard a sharp intake of air as Gunner looked at the shadow on the frame. She'd recognized it also.

'No, I'm afraid not, pal,' I said as I threw down a final shot of Jameson. I wasn't sure if it was the Jameson or what I'd just seen through the loupe that caused me to speak in a soft and husky voice, scarcely above a whisper. Maybe it was a little of both.

'It's a picture of a man murdering another man,' I said.

12

'The trouble is that it's a right-handed shadow,' I said to Ratso. We were sitting around the kitchen table at 199B Vandam waiting for the coffee to perk or for something else to happen. Whichever came first.

The coffee perked. I poured us both a cup.

'I see you're left-handed yourself,' said Ratso as he ran-sacked the kitchen looking for cream and sugar.

'You're extremely observant, my dear Ratso,' I said. 'Of course I'm left-handed. Isn't everybody left-handed?'

'I'm not left-handed,' said Ratso.

'No, you wouldn't be,' I said.

The cat jumped up on the kitchen table and began walking toward Ratso's coffee cup.

'Get down,' said Ratso to the cat. The cat didn't say anything.

'Ratso,' I said, 'just imagine that you're the guest, and the cat and I are your hosts, and we're all riding in Dr Dolittle's giant pink sea snail.'

'All right,' said Ratso, 'we're on this giant fucking pink sea snail and we're traveling back to last Thursday night to investigate the murder of Larry Barkin. What do we see?'

'We see a preponderance of left-handers, a right-handed shadow of a murderer, and a two-dollar bill.'

'Okay,' said Ratso, 'you find a two-dollar bill in Barkin's pocket at the murder scene. The Hank Williams song "Hey, Good Lookin' " comes in the mail addressed to the victim and postmarked prior to the murder. Right?'

'Right,' I said. I got up and poured us both another cup of coffee. The cat hopped off the table and onto the desk and curled up under the desk lamp. 'She's in Miami Beach,' I said.

'Who is?' asked Ratso.

'The cat,' I said.

'Now the song makes mention,' said Ratso, 'of a two-dollar bill in the lyric. "A hot rod Ford and a two-dollar bill." So whoever gave Barkin the two-dollar bill, or placed it in his pocket afterward, is the murderer and the sender of the song. But why does he want to give us this deliberate signature, this clue? Why this connection to Hank Williams?'

43

'These are deep waters, my dear Ratso, for the pink sea snail. Hank Williams has had an almost magical effect on millions of people for a great many years now. I know something about the power he can exert, even dead, over people. He's one of my patron saints, you know.'

'Really?' asked Ratso.

'Sure,' I said. 'Just like Jesus, Hitler, and Bob Dylan are your three patron saints, I have three also.'

'Oh, yeah,' said Ratso, 'who are the other two besides Hank?'

'Anne Frank and Ernie Kovacs,' I said.

'I see,' said Ratso. 'But what about Sherlock?'

'I am Sherlock,' I said.

'So who the hell am I?' Ratso asked. 'Dr Watson or Dr Dolittle?'

'Dealer's choice,' I said. 'They're the only two doctors who still make house calls.'

It was two cups of coffee later and Ratso was standing up and looking around for his coat, when the phones rang. 'Stick around a minute,' I said as I walked over to the desk and picked up the blower on the left.

It was Detective Sergeant Cooperman, and his low, grating voice was coming down the line at me like somebody's runaway bowling ball. Apparently Gunner had given him the contact sheet.

'Well,' I said into the receiver, 'maybe he kills left, photographs right.'

I won't repeat what Cooperman said to that, but the essence of his thought pattern was why was I asking everyone in New York if they were left-handed when Cooperman was right now looking at photographic evidence that clearly indicated the killer was right-handed? He said a few other things, too, then he hung up. Ratso had walked over to the refrigerator, opened the door, and was looking inside.

I had already told Ratso about the shadow on the contact sheet, and now I went into some little detail about the guitar experiment I'd done in the loft on the previous Sunday. 'You see,' I said, 'I still believe the killer's a southpaw. Something's wrong somewhere.'

'Well,' said Ratso, 'a right-handed shadow is better than no shadow at all.'

'Not if there's a left-handed lunatic running around plotting who he'll kill next,' I said.

'Oh,' said Ratso, 'so you think we'll be hearing from Hank again.'

'I'm sure of it,' I said. 'Nothing's more dangerous than the arrogance of a clever killer. And I haven't been able to prove a damn thing. The investigation's going nowhere extremely fast.'

'Don't be so hard on yourself,' said Ratso. 'You've got a negative attitude.'

I lit a cigar thoughtfully with a kitchen match. 'That's it, pal,' I said softly. 'You've just said it. I've got to get my hands on that contact sheet again. The old men playing chess in Washington Square Park.'

I walked quickly over to the far end of the loft. 'Come over here, Ratso,' I said. 'Look at that picture on the wall.' It was a framed photograph of an older man playing chess with a small boy. 'That's Samuel Reshevsky, the world grand master, when he came to Houston, Texas, and played fifty people simultaneously and beat them all. The kid was the youngest person Reshevsky played that night. I think the kid was only seven years old at the time, so this picture made the front page of the *Houston Chronicle*. Reshevsky later told the kid's dad he was very sorry to have beaten his kid, but he had to take the match seriously because losing to a seven-year-old wasn't good for a grand master's reputation.'

Ratso looked up at the picture for a while. 'So how do you know all this?' he asked.

'I was the kid,' I said.

Ratso looked at the picture again. So did I for a moment. The face reflected an innocence and a keen, childlike intensity of spirit that I no longer saw when I looked in the mirror, and I only hoped had been consigned to my heart.

'That picture,' I said, 'has something important to tell us about the shadow who murdered Larry Barkin.'

'Let me guess,' said Ratso. 'The killer comes from Houston?'

I took a few patient puffs on my cigar and I looked at Ratso. 'Not quite,' I said.

13

I spent most of Thursday trying to locate the bald-headed lawyer, but I couldn't find hide nor hair of him. It was hard to believe that nobody I'd talked to could tell me his name. That they'd all assumed he'd gotten into the dressing room with somebody else. You'd think people would pay closer attention to a bald-headed lawyer who was dispensing cocaine.

Late that afternoon I called the city desk of the *Daily News*.

'City desk,' came a busy, distracted voice.

'Is McGovern there?' I asked.

'I don't see him,' said the voice.

'Never could see McGovern,' I said. 'Well, when he gets in, will you ask him to call Holmes?'

'Will do,' said the voice. I fed the cat and fielded a brutal, unrelenting series of stray phone calls, full of sound and fury and signifying nothing except that my phone was still working and that a guy named Joe in Little Italy was delivering an espresso-cappuccino machine to my loft the following week as a token of gratitude for my helping with a little situation the previous year. I never refused tokens of gratitude. Especially when they came from Little Italy.

The other calls, in a random and haphazard order, were from Downtown Judy, who said she was coming over. I said okay. From Bill Dick at the Lone Star, wanting to know how I was progressing. I said okay. From Uptown Judy, who said she was coming down. I said okay. And from Ratso, who wanted to know what the picture of me playing chess with Samuel What's-his-name meant. I said 'Reshevsky.'

In between the calls I walked over to the kitchen window and watched the dismal darkness settle over the dismal November gray of New York City. New York was the kind of place where you could hide from anything. Possibly even yourself.

At seven-fifteen, I called the *Daily News* again. McGovern answered.

'City desk,' he said.

'Why didn't you call me, precious lips?'

'I didn't get a message from you,' said McGovern.

'I left a message for you to call Holmes. Sort of a pseudonym. Thought you might pick up on it.'

'Shit,' he said, 'the message I got was to call home. I knew that couldn't be right.' McGovern was a devoted bachelor and had lived in a small apartment on Jane Street for as long as I'd known him. He had no family living, and very little of it dead.

'You're not kiddin',' I said.

'Hey, I've got something for you,' said McGovern.

'Spit it,' I said. It was about time somebody had something for me. Not that I'd ever expected the solution of the problem to be easy. If the killer was someone I didn't know, possibly didn't even suspect, then how in the hell was I going to find him? If he was somebody that I did know, he was one pretty sick item.

'First, Flippo,' said McGovern. 'Apparently Flippo's some kind of literary ghoul. Only writes about dead people.'

'That's not so strange, McGovern,' I said. 'You told me yourself that you're the *Daily News'* number one man when it comes to writing obits for the living. That's not only ghoulish, it's cynical.'

'Yeah,' said McGovern, 'but it requires a lot of imagination. You ought to see the obit I just finished on Bob Hope. Want to hear it?'

'Maybe some other time,' I said. 'It'll keep.'

'Yeah, but will Bob?' asked McGovern.

'Back to Flippo,' I said.

'Here's part of a review on Flippo's book *Your Cheatin' Heart*: ". . . The thing that makes this work different from other books on Hank Williams is that thoughts, emotions, scenes, and incidents are herein described that only Hank Williams himself could have known." '

'That's bizarre enough to make me want to read the book,' I said. 'Of course I never took the Amelia Earhart Speed Reading Course or whatever it's called, so at my remedial pace I probably won't finish it until it's too late.'

'Too late for what?' asked McGovern.

'I'd rather not say.'

'Sure,' said McGovern. 'Top secret. Classified. I understand.' I was hoping McGovern wouldn't go into a snit. That could only slow the flow of information. And there was precious little of that as it was. 'Okay,' he said finally, 'on to Barkin.'

I felt a small wave of relief that my main source for background information was not being shut off to me.

McGovern wasn't exactly Deep Throat, but he did have remarkable access to almost any facet of American history. Right at his Irish fingertips. The wave of relief was not big enough to make me feel very good about how the case was going. It was just about enough for me to lean back and light a fresh cigar. With a Bic.

Using a Bic made it extremely difficult to keep the cigar well above the flame. I wondered what Charles Lamb would've thought about my lighting a cigar with a Bic. Of course they didn't have Bics in those days. And these days, we didn't have Charles Lamb.

'Larry Barkin and the Barkin Brothers,' said McGovern. 'Seven gold records . . . twice named country singer of the year . . . two brothers, Jim and Randy . . . born in the little Texas town of Medina . . . Christ, all country singers were born in a little Texas town.'

'Hank wasn't,' I said.

'No?'

'No, sir,' I said. 'He was born in a little town in Alabama.'

'I see,' said McGovern.

'You can skip the part about Barkin buying his mother a big house outside of Nashville,' I said.

'How'd you know he bought his mother a big house outside of Nashville?'

'All country singers buy their mothers big houses outside of Nashville.'

'You oughta be tellin' this shit to me,' said McGovern.

'Is there anything else now?' I asked. 'Any problems? Legal? Marital? Anything shady or questionable about this all-American boy?'

'Yeah,' said McGovern. 'There was a pretty ugly lawsuit about five years ago. Barkin and a former manager of his. Bit of country music mud-slinging involved.'

'Was this guy screwing Barkin?'

'Sexually? Financially? Spiritually?' asked McGovern.

'Financially, McGovern,' I said. Sexually, I doubted. And all managers screwed country singers spiritually.

'Looks like he was screwing Barkin financially. Barkin won a big settlement from the guy – the guy was also a lawyer. Not that all lawyers are crooks.'

'Of course not,' I said shortly. 'What's this lawyer's name?'

'Murray Fishkin,' said McGovern.

'Bald?'

'Come again?'

'Is the goddamn lawyer bald?'

'Just a minute. I think there's a picture here.' There was silence on the line for a few minutes while McGovern went away to flip some pages or adjust some microfilm or whatever they did. Then he came back on the line. 'As an eagle,' he said.

'Thanks, McGovern,' I said, 'I definitely owe you one.'

'Yeah, well, how about telling me what this is all about? I mean it's obvious you're looking into the Barkin murder. Let's see. Barkin was bumped off exactly a week ago at the Lone Star. Okay, I understand your involvement in that, but what's Hank Williams got to do with this mess? He's been dead for twenty-five years.'

'Thirty-three years,' I said. 'And look, I really can't tell you just now. I'm not sure I even know what the connection is myself.'

'C'mon, man,' he said. 'Give me a little hint. I'll figure it out for myself.'

McGovern and I had met on the gangplank of Noah's ark. But in a murder investigation you had to be very careful what you told old friends. Especially old friends who were members of the Fourth Estate.

'Ask Bob Hope,' I said.

14

I didn't think it'd be a good idea to put my feet up on Sergeant Cooperman's desk. The way I looked at it, just coming down to the precinct station house had been fairly testicular. I knew I wasn't going to be working hand in glove with the cops on this one, but I thought maybe I'd get a look at that contact sheet again. All I could see at the moment was Cooperman's fiery little eyes. They were boring right through me like two piss holes in the snow.

'Fox!' shouted Cooperman. Fox detached his serpentine frame from a nearby filing cabinet, walked over to the desk, put both hands down on top of it, and leaned as far as he could toward me. I could see why they called them the fuzz. If he got much closer he'd be growing out of my chin.

'What do I do with this guy?' asked Cooperman in a very soft whisper. Soft as a down pillow just before it smothered you to death. 'I call him and let him know he's screwin' up, and he takes it as an invitation to come here to the squad room for a chat.'

Cooperman eased his large body backward in his chair. He picked up a yellow pencil and tapped it slowly on the desk. Fox stood up, folded his arms across his chest, and glared down at me. The three of us held our respective positions for quite a few pencil tappings. It reminded me of a B movie. Unfortunately, it wasn't. It was a B world.

'I'd like to have a look,' I said, 'at the photographic evidence that shows the killer is right-handed.'

'Fox, get him the contact sheet,' said Cooperman. 'You look, then you leave,' he said to me. He'd stopped tapping, but his orbs were still working overtime on me.

'Fine,' I said. Cooperman lacked certain qualities that were essential in a good host.

Fox went into another room. 'Let me tell you something,

friend,' said Cooperman. He used the word 'friend' in the same way that a Turk, or an Arab, or a redneck used it when he wanted you to know you were not his friend. 'If it weren't for your pal, that manager of the club – '

'Cleve,' I said.

'Cleve,' he said, 'alibiing for you, you might just have made a prime suspect yourself.'

'Cleve called me after Barkin was croaked,' I said.

'Save it,' said Cooperman.

Fox came back in the room. He put the contact sheet on the desk and pointed demonstratively at the frame that contained the shadow. I followed the moving finger.

'Right-handed beyond a shadow of a doubt,' he said. 'You don't agree, Tex?' Fox had seen me sometime in the past when I was wearing a cowboy hat, and he'd managed to retain the image.

I wasn't looking at the shadow anymore. I was looking at the bottom of the page at the last three frames on the roll. A couple of old guys playing chess in Washington Square Park.

'No, I don't,' I said. 'I've thought for a while that something was wrong with this contact sheet. Look at this chessboard.' I held the sheet up to where both Cooperman and Fox could see.

'The black square is at each player's right-hand side,' I said.

'So what?' asked Fox.

'So the *white* square is supposed to be at each player's right-hand side.'

'We'll check on it,' said Cooperman.

'This is no time for puns, Sergeant,' I said.

Cooperman looked at me. Then he jerked his head rather violently toward the other room, and Fox took the contact sheet from the desk and walked away with it.

'What about the Hank Williams song that came in the mail?' I asked.

'You country singers got country music on the brain. We're looking into it. You see this pile right here?' Cooperman nodded his head to indicate a stack of papers on his desk. I nodded my head to indicate I could see the stack of papers. 'You know what that is?' he asked.

'You're getting an early start on your income tax?' I asked.

Cooperman smiled a sweet, smirky, patronizing little smile. Fortunately, it did not reach his eyes. 'These are twenty-four unsolved homicide cases sitting right next to a cold cup of coffee,' he said brusquely. 'Take a walk.'

I took a walk.

15

Late that night I witnessed the most exciting and harrowing experience of the week, excluding, of course, the murder of Larry Barkin. It involved the two Judys and it happened at the front door of my loft. It was a nerve-wrenching near miss. Uptown Judy was going down in the freight elevator at the same time as Downtown Judy was coming up the stairs.

One moment I was saying, 'Good night, Judy. Take care,' and twenty seconds later I was saying, 'So Judy, where the hell you been?'

Friday morning I was sitting at my desk. Both Judys had come and gone, in a manner of speaking. Neither of them was any the wiser. Neither was I. Larry Barkin was still dead, and I had the sickening suspicion that no matter what I did, I'd be barkin' up the wrong tree.

I was wearing my purple bathrobe, drinking coffee, and

opening the day's correspondence with my Smith & Wesson knife. The cat was lying on the desk under the lamp. The cat and I were engaged in a little contest. We were trying to see which of us could display the least emotion every time I opened a bill.

I was studying an invitation to a roller-skating party at a discotheque, when the phones rang. It was 11.37 a.m. I picked up the blower on the left.

'We got another one,' the voice said. It was Cleve calling from the Lone Star. There was a strange note in his voice, and it took me a moment to figure out what it was. It was what a shiver would sound like if you could hear it.

'Relax, pal,' I said. 'You got another what?'

'Another song, man,' he said. 'Another Hank Williams song came in the mail.'

16

It was pushing three in the afternoon and I was standing at the kitchen window of the loft waiting for the messenger to bring over the Hank Williams song from the Lone Star. I didn't know what the song was, or to whom it'd been sent. Cleve had been too upset to even hum a few bars. From time to time I picked up the puppet head from the top of the refrigerator and gave it a little anticipatory juggle from hand to hand, but no messenger.

Why was I waiting here? It was a gorgeous day, as we say in New York. Hell, I could've been out in the sunshine kicking the garbage around on the sidewalk.

I started to pace back and forth across the length of the loft, periodically gazing hopefully down at the sidewalk. Sometimes pacing back and forth helped me take stock of things. The cat, some years back, had followed at my heels as I paced up and down with cigar in hand. The cat had now given up such kittenish games. I continued to pace. I was a creature of narrow habit, and I was somewhat disappointed in the cat, but I never let it show. No doubt, the cat had her reasons to be disappointed in me as well. Somehow we managed.

I stopped pacing. I wasn't getting anywhere, figuratively or literally. I looked at the cat. She was curled up asleep on the rocker. The loft was as close to home as either of us was ever likely to get. It wasn't home, but how could it be? Everybody knew that home was in Kansas. And it better stay there if it knew what was good for it.

I poured a cup of coffee and prowled around the loft like a battery-powered tiger trying desperately to burn bright with a knowledge I didn't possess. What did I actually know? I thought about it for a moment. A country singer had rather unpleasantly gotten himself unsung eight days ago. Prior to the murder, someone had sent him the Hank Williams Song 'Hey, Good Lookin',' which contained the reference to a two-dollar bill in the lyrics, the same two-dollar bill having found its nefarious way into the dying breast pocket of the sequined suit of the young cowboy. Right out of the Old West. But East was East and West was West. Who'd want to croak a saccharine-tongued, good ol' boy, housewife's dream anyway? Besides myself, of course. I didn't have an answer.

And now, to show it was nothing personal against Larry Barkin, another song had arrived. The cops, according to Cleve, had dusted it for prints. Unsuccessfully. Even murderers watched enough television to know about fingerprints. The cops' interest level in the new song had, apparently, not been high. Cooperman had told Cleve and Bill Dick that there were fifteen million nut cases sitting around the New York area with nothing to do but clog the mails with letters, threats, and solicitations directed at well-known people.

I wasn't sure that Fox and Cooperman even knew who Hank Williams was. I knew Hank didn't know who Fox and Cooperman were. He'd been dead for thirty-three years.

But even that narrow little fact wasn't exactly true. In a far more important sense, Hank Williams, like Jesus or Joe Hill, in a random and haphazard order, never really died. People still listened to Hank's words and Hank's voice, and there was a magic about the man that had conquered the mortal boundaries of geography, culture, and time.

And there were people like Chet Flippo who kept Hank alive. I wondered very briefly if Flippo also could be making people dead. I didn't really believe it. He'd given the bartender a two-dollar bill at the High Five. He was a Hank Williams nut, but so was Mike Simmons. If Ratso had known a little more about country music, he'd probably be a Hank Williams nut, too. There were literally millions of them. And a Hank Williams nut was a hard nut to crack.

Flippo, in his distant, unassuming way, was a friend of mine. Was there a killer switch somewhere in that artichoke heart? I didn't see it. But then, if it were there, it wasn't the kind of thing you were likely to see.

Simmons was more hot-blooded, more frustrated, more capable of violent murder. And he was left-handed. He loved Hank Williams more than God. 'You'd throw Hank fucking Williams out of here,' he'd shouted to the philistines at City Limits. A revealing line, I thought. But it was too flimsy a line even to snort from the smooth, domed top of Murray Fishkin's head.

And what of Fishkin? The mysterious lawyer-manager-crook whose reputation and profile were both lower than a whale turd? I'd have to get on to him. When the law offices opened on Monday morning, I'd open him like a forty-two-cent can of cat food. Where there's a will, there's a lawyer.

I even wondered about Gunner, the trusty girl photographer. There was something about her that didn't quite fit the picture. And for some reason I trusted her even less than I trusted most attractive women I'd met. Was it just male chauvinist prejudice? Was it? Maybe it was male intuition. No, it couldn't be that. Everybody knew there was no such thing. Okay. Who was left? Had to be left . . .

I heard a shout from below and I threw down the puppet head on the parachute. I watched it as it glided gracefully down to the sidewalk. It was really a thing of beauty to see.

Moments later I heard a continuous rapping at the door of the loft. It was either a very insistent person or a pretty tall woodpecker. And by this time I didn't care which as long as it was carrying a Hank Williams song in its beak. I opened the door.

'You Kinky?' asked the messenger. In his right hand was a manila envelope, and in his left was a large carton that looked like it could hold more ice cream than I wanted to think about. I nodded. 'What's in the carton?' I asked.

'Man said it was Five-Alarm Chili,' he said.

'That Bill Dick thinks of everything,' I said. 'And now, the envelope, please.' He handed me the envelope and I took it over to the desk.

'Come on in,' I said. 'I may want to send this back where it came from.' The messenger came in and stood by the door.

'Pour yourself some coffee or something,' I said. The guy wasn't doing anything, but sometimes it's more annoying to have somebody not doing something than it is to have somebody doing something really obnoxious.

I looked at the outside of the envelope. Same big block

letters as before. But this time it was addressed to Bubba and Blane, c/o The Lone Star Cafe.

Bubba and Blane Borgelt were two big friendly Texas brothers with a string of catchy country hits as long as their tour bus. I'd even worked a few shows with them on the road. What I liked to call the early days. 'When Jesus was our savior and cotton was our king,' as Billy Joe Shaver put it. 199B Vandam was still a warehouse back then. I didn't have a cat. I didn't even have intimations of an espresso machine.

I opened the envelope. It contained the sheet music for the Hank Williams song 'Settin' the Woods on Fire.' If I remembered correctly, Bubba and Blane were playing the Lone Star on Monday night.

'Watcha got there?' asked the messenger.

'Somebody's swan song,' I said.

17

On Saturday afternoon Ratso and I were sitting in the Carnegie Delicatessen on Seventh Avenue and Fifty-fifth Street. Outside it was snowing. The Carnegie Deli was a good spiritual place to be when it was snowing. So was a bar. Or any place in the Village. Actually, when it snowed in New York, every block took on the aspects of a little village. The snow blocked out the tall buildings and seemed to bring people closer together. It created a blanket of peace and tranquility over the city. Strangers talked to one another. You almost felt like you were in a small town. Fortunately, it never lasted.

I was working on a matzo ball about the size of McGovern's head and looking forward to renewing my acquaintance with Bubba and Blane on Monday night. I didn't think, however, that I should get too attached. Ratso was eating a large number of pickles from one of the buckets that were always on the tables. Leo had brought us linen napkins, treatment reserved only for celebrities and special friends.

'What did you order, Ratso?' I asked. The matzo ball was killer bee.

'Pope's nose,' he said.

'What the hell's a pope's nose?' I asked.

'Turkey's ass,' he said.

Ratso handled several pickles in the bucket, and finally settled on one that met his culinary approval.

'Ratso, I don't want to put you off your appetite for your pope's nose,' I said, 'but I'd like for you to look over something with me.' I took the sheet music out of my coat pocket.

We looked over the lyrics together to 'Settin' the Woods on Fire.' They were as follows:

> Comb your hair and paint and powder
> You act proud and I'll act prouder
> You sing loud and I'll sing louder
> Tonight we're settin' the woods on fire
>
> You're my gal and I'm your feller
> Dress up in your frock of yeller
> I'll look swell but you'll look sweller
> Settin' the woods on fire
>
> We'll take in all the honky-tonks, tonight
> We're havin' fun
> We'll show the folks a brand new dance
> That never has been done
>
> I don't care who thinks we're silly
> You be daffy and I'll be dilly

59

We'll order up two bowls of chili
Settin' the woods on fire

I'll gas up my hot rod stoker
We'll get hotter than a poker
You'll be broke but I'll be broker
Tonight we're settin' the woods on fire.

'The song's a field day for a criminal mind,' said Ratso, shaking his head in a disbelieving manner. He reached around in the bucket for another pickle.

'It's not all that bad,' I said. 'You see, I don't think the murderer is actually revealing his methodology with these songs. How he's going to do it, why he's going to do it, we don't know. All we know for sure is he's going to do it. And there'll be a clue in the song that connects it to the crime. He's playing with us. He's inviting us. What we're looking at is really the killer's calling card. The fact that he uses ol' Hank as his vessel of communication may be the most revealing thing we know yet about the person we're looking for.'

'Let's look at the song,' said Ratso. 'Okay . . . here – "We'll get hotter than a poker." What about that?'

'My dear Ratso, ' I said, 'this is not an English hunting lodge. This is New York City.'

'Right, Sherlock,' he said. 'I forgot.' He looked down at the song again. 'How about this? Two bowls of chili. "We'll order up two bowls of chili." '

'So don't eat the chili,' I said.

'Hell,' said Ratso, 'the regular chili at the Lone Star could kill you.'

'Not a chance,' I said. 'You're just an urban woosy, Ratso. But I need you there Monday night. You bring a kind of naïveté to the investigation that already is suggesting certain possibilities to me.'

'You're a pope's nose,' he said.

As we got into the cab to go back downtown, Ratso told the driver to hurry, he was late. 'Everybody's late,' said the driver as he threw the meter. 'In this town, everybody's late.'

I looked out the window of the hack and watched the snowy sidewalks slide past in a dream. I wasn't late yet. But I was starting to run scared. And I had a feeling Monday night was going to come faster than a nymphomaniac.

18

Cleve was the first person I saw at the door of the Lone Star on Monday night. He was wringing his hands like an unctuous funeral director. I had a few words with him, walked over to the downstairs bar, and took a seat on the only empty barstool – right next to the cash register. The businessman's piano.

I ordered a Jameson and looked around for either strange or familiar faces. I didn't see any. Everybody at the downstairs bar looked vaguely familiar. Like you could almost place them but you didn't really want to. They looked like people who habitually shopped the generic aisle of the supermarket. Maybe some of it had rubbed off on them.

I turned around on the barstool and watched the opening act. I'd seen this band thousands of times over the years. Different places, different faces, same old song. Their current favorite was 'Luckenbach, Texas.' Probably once it had been 'Bad, Bad Leroy Brown' or 'Are You Going to San Francisco?' if they'd been old enough to go, and it looked like they had been. They'd always changed, if not with the times, then just a little bit behind them. They'd learned to 'roll with the bullets,' as my friend Doug Kenney used to say before he fell off his perch in Hawaii. I missed Doug. I signaled to the bartender for another Jameson, and when he poured it I didn't miss Doug so much.

The band was going through the torturous twenty minutes of musical foreplay that is sometimes known as tuning up. Should take under a minute, but these guys wanted all the stage time they could get. Didn't want to leave a rhinestone unturned in the limelight. What the hell. Wherever there were barflies there had to be lounge lizards. It was a law of nature.

I turned back to the bar and finished my drink. Why was I being so hard on these guys? They were just trying to earn a living. 'Hell, everybody can't be Hank Williams,' I said. 'Everybody can't die in the backseat of a Cadillac on the way to Canton, Ohio.'

'What was that?' asked the bartender.

'Put it on the tab,' I said.

The band had started to play and I had started for the stairs to the balcony. It gave a better view of the whole place and it wasn't quite as loud. Nothing on the planet was quite as loud as sitting at the downstairs bar of the Lone Star Cafe and listening to a country rock band.

The second floor of the Lone Star was usually where most of the action was, always discounting, of course, the executive men's room. I wasn't halfway up the stairs before I regretted not having had a few more drinks before attaining that second Dantean level. Somebody was yelling 'Kinkstah! Kinkstah!' at me. Once you heard that voice you never forgot it. It was Ratso. I'd wanted to keep a slightly lower profile, but I now saw that was going to be rather difficult.

Ratso was holding forth with some people at a table on the far side of the balcony. I gave him a little Hitler wave, like an Italian waiter carrying a tray, except without the tray. It was a gesture that clearly indicated 'Cut me some slack, pal,' but as I reached the second-floor landing I heard the dread macawlike tones once more. 'Kinkstah . . . Kinkstah!' I chose to ignore them for the moment. I had to because I ran right into Mike Simmons at the top of the stairs. I'd been trying to turn left and he'd come charging out of the ladies' room at the top of the stairs. There were angry shouts emanating from the ladies' room and Mike seemed a little out of breath.

'Sure isn't Marylou's,' he said. 'They've got a much more progressive attitude over there.' Simmons had been known to enter ladies' rooms occasionally and offer the ladies controlled substances if they would take their blouses off. It worked about half the time. The other half it could get pretty ugly.

'Mike, I don't have any strong moral feelings about this one way or the other,' I said. 'I just wish you wouldn't come scooting out of there like a goddamn dog.'

'I'll try to remember that,' he said. It looked like he'd already had the drinks I needed. We walked over to the upstairs bar for a couple more. I couldn't see Simmons killing anybody but himself. And he'd been working on that for a long time. Hadn't we all.

I thought I'd have one drink with Simmons, check out the upstairs bar area and gift shop, and then join Ratso at the table he was holding on the balcony rail. It gave a good overview of the whole place.

Security looked pretty good. Patrick, the bouncer, was circulating like a rather large, anxious society hostess; Norman, the sweet-voiced and obviously very dangerous, androgynous black belt, was standing at the top of the stairs. When Norman smiled, it was obvious that he was pretty ill. His smile told you he'd love to dice up your Adam's apple for kicks. Mal, the former cop who ran a limo service on the side, stopped by the bar to take a little topper off my drink.

'Have a nice day,' he said.

I lit a cigar. Simmons went to the men's room on the right of the bar if you were facing away from the bar on a barstool, which I was. I puffed thoughtfully on the cigar as I watched a cowboy from New Jersey. He'd had a long ride over to the Lone Star that night. Probably somebody's dope dealer. Ridin' 'cross the desert on a horse with no legs.

I downed the Jameson and let my mind wander the range a bit. Visions of two-dollar bills, left-handed swingers, Hank Williams songs. I thought of what Hank must have looked and sounded like playing the Grand Ol' Opry those many years ago. A troubled, leaning Jesus who sang with the sadness of a train and the beauty of a whippoorwill. It was said that on a number of occasions he'd actually cried while he sang on that stage. Over two decades later I played the Grand Ol' Opry myself a few times. I remembered walking on the stage in front of thousands of people at the old Ryman Auditorium looking for Hank's teardrops. But they, like my own, had long since dried. At least that's what I thought at the time.

I looked up just as a blinding light flashed in my eyes. I heard the sound of British laughter. Reticent, almost clipped.

'Very unprofessional of me, I'm afraid,' said Gunner as she put her camera down on the bar next to me.

'Very tedious,' I said. It was always hard to look indignant in the face of a beautiful face.

'You were such a study in . . . in introspection,' she said. 'Where were you just now when I took the picture?'

'Oh, Nashville,' I said. 'Nashville and Vancouver.'

'That's a long way to travel on a barstool,' she said softly.

I downed the fresh shot of Jameson that the bartender had poured. 'I get around,' I said.

The opening band was still thrashing through their first set as I took Gunner up the back stairs. They led up to the third-floor dressing rooms. As a performer myself, I was always hesitant about bugging entertainers just before a show. This time I was prepared to make an exception to my rule. Bubba and Blane might not be around afterward.

'The security people were very sweet,' said Gunner. 'They let me take a photograph.'

'I let you take a photograph, too,' I said.

'You couldn't have stopped me if you'd wanted to,' she said tauntingly. Beneath the royal blue of her eyes I saw more than a taunt. More than laughter. I saw a challenge to mankind.

'Who would want to?' I asked admiringly. She nodded her head once in agreement.

We walked down the little hall on the third floor and I knocked on the dressing room door. A big Nashville type with long sideburns and a Billy Graham hairdo opened the door.

'They're okay,' Cleve shouted to him from the far side of the room.

'That's good to know,' I said to Gunner. We walked in and the guy closed the door behind us. Bill Dick was standing next to Cleve and talking with Bubba and Blane. Patrick, the bouncer, had attached himself to the wall by the door like a red-bearded barnacle. He nodded at me. There were several other people in the room busy seeing and being seen. I didn't know who they were. A table of drinks had been set up by the open door to the patio. I looked through the door and could see the green metal scales of the iguana gleaming in the cold moonlight. Gunner followed my gaze and shivered slightly.

'Cold?' I asked.

'No,' she said. 'I was just thinking . . .'

'Well, don't do it again,' I said. 'Thinking can be dangerous. At least I think it can.' The mood in the room was quiet. Maybe a little tense. That could just be opening-night jitters, I thought. Especially for country acts, playing New York City and the Lone Star Cafe was a big thing. It didn't mean a flying Canadian to me, though. When you live close to the pyramids you become acclimated to them.

I walked over to the table with the drinks and procured a couple. If Gunner didn't want one I'd drink two. As I walked over to the Borgelts, Bill Dick went over to Gunner. Club owners like to rub shoulders with the stars, but even more than that, they like to rub anything they can with pretty girls. Some people who don't own clubs like to do that, too.

I shook hands with Blane and Bubba. A few guys in the band were tuning up instruments over in a corner, getting ready for the first set. 'Long time between dreams,' I said.

'Haven't seen you in a coon's age,' said Bubba.

'In a coon's age,' agreed Blane.

'Let's keep race out of it, boys,' I said. Blane laughed. Bubba adjusted his 'Go Texas' bow tie with the two sequined strands of material running down his chest. The bow tie was a clip-on job. Smart after what had happened to Larry Barkin. I took out a cigar and lit it. Then I took out two more cigars and offered one to each of the Borgelts. They both turned them down. Almost everybody did. That's why I offered them to people.

'You guys nervous?' I asked.

'About the show?' Bubba asked.

'About the other thing,' I said ominously. 'Why the hell did you guys take this gig? If I'm not being too personal.'

'Just a crackpot,' laughed Bubba. 'You can't hide from life. Besides, a gig's a gig.'

'Can't hide from life,' said Blane. 'A gig's a gig.' Sounded like he'd spent too many years in the echo chamber.

'That's the spirit,' said Bill Dick as he hurried back over and put one arm around each of the boys. 'How about a few shots, Gunner?'

Gunner obligingly shot away. At Dick's request I got into the act and stood next to Bubba. Then Cleve slipped in next to Blane. Pretty soon everybody'd gotten into the picture but Mother Maybelle Carter. That was country music, all right. One big happy family. Almost.

When my eyes came back into focus again I saw two blurry figures lurking in the doorway of the dressing room. Fox and Cooperman. Gunner had stopped taking pictures but Dick still had his arms around Bubba and Blane.

'I'd like to see somebody try something tonight,' he said.

19

Gunner and I joined the Ratso table on the balcony rail. Ratso's date for the evening was porn star Annie Sprinkle. She wore her wristwatch around her ankle and her heart on her sleeve. Sometimes that was all she wore.

We had survived two brutal sets by the opening act, and one moderately entertaining show by Bubba and Blane. We'd been up to the dressing room one more time. More drinks. More pictures. More hand-shaking, more hugging, more rubbing shoulders with the stars. Nobody'd ordered two bowls of chili.

Now we were back at the table on the balcony waiting for the final set by Bubba and Blane. A new sound man was working. He was setting up the stage for the Borgelts. Cleve stopped by our table. 'Where's Round Man the Sound Man?' I asked. He was the club's regular sound man. Weighed in at close to three hundred pounds.

'Let him have the night off,' said Cleve. 'This guy's a little green, but he'll get the levels set perfect just about the time the show's over.' He smiled.

'Hey,' he said, 'your buddy Flippo was asking about you. He's in the gift shop setting up a display for his book.'

'I'll just see what he wants,' I said, getting up to leave.

'I'll just keep an eye on Gunner for you,' said Cleve.

Flippo was autographing somebody's book in the gift shop. 'Be careful,' I told the young woman whose book he was signing, 'his autographs are bouncing.'

'Hey,' said Flippo, 'just who I was looking for. How's the book going?' It was moving about as fast as the Barkin murder case, but I had to say something.

'The thing that makes it work,' I said, 'is that it contains thoughts, incidents, scenes, emotions that only Hank Williams himself could have known.'

'Glad you're enjoying it,' said Flippo.

'Yeah,' I said. 'Look. The other night at the High Five when you gave me the book – where'd you get that two-dollar bill you had?'

'Larry gave it to me,' he said. 'Larry Barkin.'

'Fine,' I said. I went back to the table. Cleve was gone, but Simmons had taken his place. The Borgelts were coming on to the stage to raucous applause from the crowd. I pulled up an empty chair from another table and sat down. A waitress came by and we ordered a fresh round of drinks and sat back to watch the show.

Bubba Borgelt was at center mike. He played lead guitar and sang. Blane was on the mike at his right. He sang harmony. Sometimes the two would get together on the center mike, and the vocals really came across then. The sound man was beginning to get his act together. The band – a drummer, bass player, fiddler, and steel player – were all smooth, slick, right out of Nashville central casting.

68

'They ain't the Everly Brothers,' said Ratso, 'but they're not bad.'

'Their long suit's recording,' I shouted over the next song. 'Their studio work's very commercial. Neither one of them's exactly Mr Charismo onstage.'

'They're not Kinky, that's for sure,' said Ratso.

'Who is?' I asked.

'Good question,' said Ratso.

'I've got to water my iguana,' said Simmons as he got up and headed for the men's room.

Gunner took a few shots of the band with the camera balanced on the rail, looking right down at the stage. We had a pretty good view of the whole club from where we sat. I gazed into the crowd on the first-floor level and I thought I saw the gleam of a bald head. It was either Daddy Warbucks or Fishkin, Barkin's former manager. I slipped out of my chair and headed around the balcony to the stairs. I took the stairs down to the first floor at a fast clip. The band was playing a country rock tune and I came close enough to the stage to touch Blane Borgelt.

I stood to the right side of the stage and looked carefully over the audience.

'Sit down,' shouted an angry woman.

'Relax, lady,' I said. I walked farther back into the club. The only familiar face I saw was Cooperman's. He gave me a grudging nod.

'You see a bald-headed guy come by this way a minute ago?' I asked.

'No,' said Cooperman. 'What happened? He snatch your handbag?'

'Look, Sergeant, as long as we're here like this, I'd like to know something.'

'I'll bet you would,' he said with just this side of a snarl.

'If something happens tonight – ' I started to say.

'It won't,' he said. He didn't look at me.

'If it does though,' I continued, 'that's two songs and two murders, right?' I figured even Cooperman could tally that up.

'Enjoy the music,' he said.

I walked back to the table. The band was into their last song. It was after two in the morning.

When I got back Gunner wasn't there. 'Your bird has flown,' said Ratso. 'She said she'd call you later in the week.'

'Great,' I said. The band had left the stage, but the hard-core crowd had gathered around on the dance floor below us and was pushing for an encore. There was a double shot of Jameson and a cold Lone Star beer at my place at the table. 'Compliments of Bill Dick,' said Ratso. 'He stopped by the table when you were away. He was damn relieved that the Borgelts made it through the night.'

'He thinks we dodged the bullet, eh?' I took a healthy jolt of the Jameson. I smiled at Annie. She smiled at me.

'Sure looks that way,' said Ratso. 'If there ever was a bullet.'

'There was one,' I said. 'Let's hope we don't have to bite it.' The band came back on the stage for the encore. 'Hey, Annie,' I said. 'I've been meaning to ask you. Why do you wear your wristwatch on your ankle?'

She looked up at me and laughed, her eyes a study in prurience and innocence. 'What a strange thing to ask,' she said.

Bubba Borgelt had come up to the center microphone, and a soft light was falling on him. He was saying what a great time we'd all had at the Lone Star tonight. He was thanking everybody in New York for being so beautiful.

'Shows what he knows,' said Ratso. I was wondering

what the hell time it was, but I didn't really want to ask Annie.

Bubba had one hand lazily draped over the neck of his guitar, and he reached out with the other to bring the microphone closer to him. The next thing I knew he was jumping around the stage like an epileptic shaman from New Guinea. He was still holding the guitar and the microphone, or rather they were still holding him. For maybe fifteen seconds everybody in the place froze like players in a macabre tableau. Everybody but Bubba.

For what seemed like an eternity, a crackling, popping noise emitted from the house speakers at a high decibel level. It didn't sound like country rock. A figure darted across the front of the stage to the soundboard where the new sound man was sitting, staring at the stage like a hypnotized puppet. The whole place was plunged into blackness except for little pinpoints of light made by people holding cigarettes. The points of light did not move. Nothing moved. It looked like the Old Chisholm Trail on a starry night, I remember thinking.

When the lights came back on, Cleve was standing by the wall switch he'd thrown to cut the juice and end the horrifying spectacle. His face was very white.

There was a smell in the place like tires burning, only not so heavy and a little sweeter. It stayed with you. The sound was something you weren't likely to forget either. Sounded like a short-order cook working overtime on a large order of french fries. But it had killed everybody's appetite.

And it had killed Bubba Borgelt.

20

Somewhere around eight-thirty Tuesday morning the phone rang by my bed. I'd been dreaming of somebody nice. Somebody from long ago. I'd been in several movies with her. Lots of excitement. A few memorable love scenes. The kind you could pop into the VCR unit you are sometimes pleased to call your brain, and play again and again and again . . .

Where was she now? In the bone orchard pushing up somebody's state flower. If they had state flowers in Canada. Like Al Capone once said: 'I don't even know what street Canada's on.'

No, they didn't seem to be making those kinds of movies anymore. What the hell. You couldn't expect more out of Hollywood than you could out of life. . . .

On about the fifth ring I collared the blower with some intensity. 'Start talkin',' I said.

The voice on the phone was shouting, kind of like a football chant. It was Ratso. The chant went as follows: 'Dim sum! Dim sum! Numbah one! Numbah one! Dim sum!' I had heard the chant before. It meant that Ratso was up early and feeling pretty good and wanted me to join him for dim sum, which was a form of Chinese breakfast. The location of the proposed breakfast was apparently the Number One Chinese Restaurant on Canal Street in Chinatown. It was my morning office when I was in Chinatown. In the afternoon, my office was Big Wong's on Mott Street. Actually, my office was anyplace that had a phone and a halfway hygienic dumper.

I looked at the clock. It was still eight-thirty.

'You participant-observers of life got it made, Ratso,' I said. 'Last night you see a guy deep-fried on a stage right in front of you, this morning you're ready to eat braised duck feet.' Actually, I was getting kind of hungry myself.

'That's what I want to talk to you about,' said Ratso. 'Last night. We'll get the morning papers and you bring that song with you, "Settin' the Trees on Fire." '

' "Settin' the Woods on Fire," ' I said.

'Yeah, that's the song.'

'Ratso, that sheet music is now evidence in a homicide. It wouldn't be exactly prudent for me to go schlepping it all over New York. The cops'll be wanting it back now.'

'What? They check it for prints yet?'

'Yeah, Starsky, they did,' I said.

'Then bring the song,' he said. 'Maybe we'll find the clue.'

'Maybe you'll find a pearl in your bean curd,' I said.

The idea of a dim sum postmortem with Ratso was not something you'd want to look forward to every morning. But if you were going to have a dim sum postmortem with Ratso, Number One was the best place to go.

I walked up Vandam to Sixth Avenue. There was still some snow around, but it wasn't the kind you see in the storybooks. It was black and gray and it had cheap wine bottles, dog turds, and off-track betting forms in it. Make a pretty unpleasant-looking snowman.

I crossed Sixth Avenue, leaned left, and continued the few blocks up Prince Street where Ratso lived. Past a day-care center, an Italian bakery, and an all-night moonie vegetable stand, in case you had to have a rutabaga at four o'clock in the morning. It was a nice neighborhood. If you liked neighborhoods.

I walked into Ratso's building and pushed his buzzer.

'Who's there?' he asked.

'Son of Sam,' I said pleasantly.

'Be right down, Son,' he said.

When Ratso came down he was wearing his coonskin cap without the tail, and he was walking very fast. 'C'mon,' he said, 'we'll pick up the papers at Bennie's, then we'll catch a cab to Chinatown.'

Ratso was walking so fast that I found myself walking behind him a good bit of the time. 'Ratso,' I said, 'slow the hell down, will you. I feel like a baby duck walking here behind you.'

'That's called imprinting,' said Ratso. 'Ask a psychologist.'

'*You* ask a psychologist,' I said.

We went into Bennie's, where Ratso bought all three newspapers: the *Post*, which I always read and Ratso hated, *The New York Times*, which Ratso loved and I didn't believe in, and the *Daily News*, which we both read to see if the Russians were attacking the Alamo yet.

Bennie always treated Ratso like Frank Sinatra when he came in the place. Ratso loved it. Bought three papers there every morning. That was probably why Bennie treated him like Frank Sinatra.

As we headed toward West Broadway, Ratso carrying the *Times* and the *Daily News* and me carrying the *Post*, I said, 'They really treat you like Frank Sinatra in there, Ratso.'

'Yeah,' he said.

'You know, Ratso,' I said, 'ol' Bennie could be camping with the clan of the dimly lit. Maybe he thinks you *are* Frank Sinatra.'

Ratso considered it for a moment. 'I tell you what,' he said. 'Don't spoil it for him.'

21

'What city?' asked the information operator.

'That's what they all say,' I said.

'What *city*, sir?'

'Nashville. For Randy Barkin.' From the pay phone where I was standing, I watched a baby squid go from Ratso's chopsticks into his mouth.

'The number is 589–2328,' said an electronic voice with about the same amount of animation as the information operator. You couldn't blame the operator, though. Imagine living out your days and finally, on your deathbed, looking back and your whole life flashing before you, and all you see is you sitting on your ass saying, 'What city?'

I put the quarter back in the phone and dialed the Nashville number.

'Thank you for using AT&T,' said the operator.

'Yeah,' I said. 'I'd like to charge this call to my office. That's 688–4070.'

'And your name, sir?'

'Ratso,' I said.

'Will you spell that, sir?' I looked over and saw Ratso eating a chicken's foot with his hand. They were kind of hard to nab with the chopsticks unless you knew what you were doing.

'R-A-T-S-O,' I said.

'Thank you, Mr Ratso. Just a moment, please.' I figured I'd charge the call to *National Lampoon*. Let him carry his own weight a little on this deal.

I waited. A number of Chinese men in business suits passed by me on the way to the men's room. A guy in white overalls came by with a dead pig on his shoulder.

'Go ahead,' said the operator.

'Randy! Leap sideways, hoss. This is Kinky.'

'Hey, brother, how are you?' said Randy in a sleepy voice. No matter how they overdubbed and remixed it, Nashville would always sound sleepy next to New York. Nashville had other things going for it. Pat Boone was from Nashville.

'Look, Randy,' I said, 'this may be important. It also may be nothing. What was the deal with your brother always carrying two-dollar bills?'

'Oh, that,' said Randy. 'He started that sort of as a gimmick with disc jockeys and fans. He'd give 'em a two-dollar bill for good luck, I guess, and to remember him by. He stopped doing that a long time ago, though.

'I remember one time he gave one to a colored street preacher, and the colored preacher said, "Bless you, child" – he didn't even know who Larry was, you see – "and may the baby Jesus hold you in the palm of His little hand." We all said "Amen" to that.'

'Yeah, that's nice,' I said. The only thing wrong with Southern Baptists was they didn't hold them underwater long enough.

'It was almost like bein' in church,' said Randy.

'Yeah,' I said, 'I can imagine.' A woman came by hustling a tray of octopus beaks or something. I didn't get a good look at it.

'Where you callin' from?' he asked. I looked across the sea of Chinese faces placidly reading Chinese newspapers and eating chicken feet in the heart of the swirling madness that was New York City.

'Far away,' I said.

22

One would think that Bubba Borgelt's demise would be a hard act to follow. But I was afraid that the killer was going to try. I was basing my judgment on the viciousness of both crimes, and the macabre nature of the 'clue' I believed I saw in 'Settin' the Woods on Fire.'

Trouble was, I was a day late and a two-dollar bill short. I knew the clue but I didn't know the killer. Or rather I knew the killer but I didn't know that I knew him.

In the words of Hank Williams, I was going to have to piece together 'a picture from life's other side.' It was hard enough to know what you were doing on this side.

I just didn't want to take a disastrous wrong turn this

early in the game. You may think that two stiffs in two weeks is not early in the game. But if you think that, believe me, you've taken a disastrous wrong turn somewhere. Pull over to life's other side and look in your glove box for your topographic map of the criminal mind. Anyone capable of doing murder, of consciously crossing those human boundaries that demark the lives of civilized men, was probably just beginning to get his second wind. And it looked like he might be going to blow Bill Dick's house down.

I stood at the window. I paced up and down. I sat at the desk. Finally, I had a heart-to-heart talk with the cat. What do we really know? The killer has sent two songs. He's killed the recipient of each. Each one a country singer performing at the Lone Star. The killer is left-handed. Knows enough about electrical wiring to arrange for a short in the system. Knows Hank Williams backward and forward. Every nuance of every lyric. He has a terminally ill sense of humor. He's very good at what he does. Any clues he's left, he's left intentionally. No face. No name. No apparent motive. And one more thing. He's got a cold, cold heart.

'What do you think?' I asked the cat. The cat didn't think too much of it apparently, because she yawned and went back to sleep.

'That's what I think, too,' I said. Neither of us knew at the time that we were getting very close to him. And soon, standing up on two legs, he would turn on us with the furious, unspeakable evil of a trapped rat.

23

Friday may have been the end of the week, but it was the beginning of a nightmare. Not that the two previous weeks had been egg creams. But things could get worse.

They did.

I was in the middle of a fitful dream Friday morning when a persistent honking from the street woke me up. I dreamed that I'd found a little baby on the sidewalk out in front of Village Cigars. It was much smaller than a baby should be. Maybe four inches long, with a diaper about the size of a commemorative stamp.

I'd picked the baby up and was holding it in my hand when a large group of familiar faces began to gather around me. Both Uptown and Downtown Judys were standing there together like demented Doublemint twins. Bill Dick was an admiral. Ratso was in his usual Sonny Bono hand-me-downs. Cleve, like a presidential assistant, was trying to keep the press away from me and the ridiculously small baby. Flippo was an SS officer. There was a guy with a haircut like Harpo Marx. He was offering cocaine to Sergeant Cooperman and Sergeant Fox, who were walking side by side, swinging their nightsticks in sync with each other.

Gunner was the Red Queen. She was carrying a gigantic tray upon which were two miniature bowls of chili, one for me and one for the baby. Mike Simmons stood a little off to the side. He wore a big white hat over his thin face. His shoulders were slightly hunched as if over a microphone. He was wearing a resplendent cowboy outfit that reflected the sun like a million tiny mirrors. For a brief moment I got a glimpse of him, and then the light became too bright. He looked like the spitting image of Hank Williams.

McGovern was dressed in a David Copperfield cap and ragged clothes. He resembled a giant newspaper boy, and in fact he was holding up a newspaper and shouting something I couldn't hear. Then my eye caught the headline. It read EXTRA! KINKY MURDERED AT LONE STAR! There was a big smile on McGovern's face.

The crowd was getting out of hand. They were all beginning to close in on me. I feared for the safety of the child. The crowd began chanting a rising, deafening chorus in unison. They shouted: 'Change the diaper! Change the diaper! Change the diaper!'

Finally, Sergeant Cooperman worked his way through the crowd to where I was standing. He slapped his nightstick into the palm of his hand two or three times. The sound echoed loudly throughout the city of New York. Then, in a surprisingly gentle voice, Cooperman spoke to me. 'What's the meaning of this?' he asked. 'What's the meaning of this?'

I didn't know what the hell it meant. All I knew was that somebody was honking his horn and it sounded like his car was double-parked in my bedroom.

I got out of bed, put on my purple bathrobe, and walked over to the kitchen window in the general direction of the honking.

I opened the window. The honking was coming from a car that someone had driven right up onto the sidewalk directly in front of 199B Vandam. The car had a green Kojak bubble light on the dash.

'Ah, Christ,' I said. The cat jumped up on the windowsill. 'What do they want with us, now?' I asked the cat as I held her in place with both hands.

I put the cat back inside on the floor and I leaned out the window. A van pulled up onto the sidewalk behind the car. It was either a very dirty white, or else beige before the pigeons had found it. On the side was some kind of emblem and the words CITY OF NEW YORK HOUSING AUTHORITY. Below that it said FOR OFFICIAL USE ONLY. Maybe they were coming to arrest the lesbian dance class, I thought.

Two very serious, very large men in suits and ties got out of the van. My normal everyday New York paranoia began to kick in. Paranoia was just a protective device that nature gave to anyone living in the city. Who were these guys, I wondered? Cossacks? Gestapo? Amway representatives?

The two guys were looking up at me now. They didn't smile or wave. What the hell did they want at this hour of the morning? I couldn't imagine. I didn't think I had any overdue parking tickets. I didn't even think I had a car.

I was subletting the loft, on a long-term basis, from an unpleasant Greek woman who liked me about as much as spiders. The only thing she asked of me was that I water her plants. That was the only thing I always forgot to do. Sometimes I thought of my cigar smoke as a form of incense to clear out her remaining bad vibrational traces. But she and I were locked in kind of a New York rental death dance. At the prices I was paying, she couldn't throw me out without cutting her own throat. Maybe the landlord had gotten wise to the sublet situation and was putting me and the cat out in the street. Who could I call? Couldn't call the cops. Couldn't call the housing authority . . .

Finally, a familiar figure stepped out of the car. It looked up at me and shouted: 'So throw down the fuckin' puppet head!'

It was Rambam. He was an old friend of mine who'd spent a couple of years on the inside. Not inside his apartment. Inside federal Never-Never-Land. Rambam was a private investigator. He was always flashing a license, but nobody ever got the chance to look at it closely. He claimed he was still wanted in every state that begins with an *I*. He knew people even Ratso never dreamed of. He had connections many people didn't even want.

I threw down the puppet head.

The two guys took a coffinlike arrangement covered with a tarp out of the back of the van. Moments later, all three of them and the large mysterious object were at my door.

'Meet your new espresso machine,' said Rambam.

The two guys brought it in and began setting it up in the kitchen. It was big, bronze, and shiny like the kind you see in Italian restaurants. It had a bronze eagle perched on top of it.

'Jesus,' I said, 'that must have set somebody back a bundle.'

'I don't think so,' said Rambam with a short laugh. 'You remember that girl you saved in the bank?'

'You mean COUNTRY SINGER PLUCKS VICTIM FROM MUGGER?' I asked.

'That's the one,' he said. 'Well, her father-in-law is Joe the Hyena.'

'That's nice,' I said. What else could I say?

'He wanted you to have this. These are two of Joe the Hyena's sons. They don't speak much English. They're fresh off the boat.'

'The Love Boat?' I asked.

'Christ, that's funny,' said Rambam. He said something in Italian to the two guys, they adjusted a few knobs on the machine, and then they nodded and left.

'I didn't know you could speak Italian, Rambam,' I said.

'Just a few phrases here and there,' he said.

'What'd you just tell Joe the Hyena's sons?' I asked. I lit up my first cigar of the morning and took a few tentative puffs.

' "Get the van back," ' he said. He loaded the machine with a bag of ground coffee beans marked 'Special Italian Roast.' He adjusted a few more gadgets, dusted the eagle with his hand, and we both leaned back against the counter to see what would happen.

Nothing happened for a while. Rambam, the cat, and I were all watching the machine. 'C'mon baby,' said Rambam, 'talk to me.'

'Maybe it speaks Japanese,' I said.

'This machine?' asked Rambam incredulously. 'You kiddin'?' The machine began to hiss and hum a little. Then it started to gurgle. Then it was off to the races. 'Smell that espresso,' said Rambam. 'Machine's worth it already. Kills the cigar smoke in here.'

Heavy cigar smoking and what I liked to think of as social usage of cocaine had fairly well destroyed my beezer. But I could smell the espresso. 'Smells great,' I said. 'First thing I've smelled in seven years.'

Rambam and I sat down at the table with two cups of steaming espresso. 'Good as the Caffé Roma any day,' he said.

'Have to do without the lemon peel,' I said.

'We'll rough it,' said Rambam. He reached in his coat pocket and took out a folded copy of the *Daily News*. He handed it to me. 'Looks like your pal Bill Dick's in trouble,' he said. 'Nobody's going to want to play his club.'

'Yeah,' I said. I opened the paper to the front page, and the first thing I saw was McGovern's by-line. The story carried the headline:

HANK WILLIAMS MURDERS
TWO SONGS – TWO SLAIN

It was inevitable that McGovern would stumble on to the fact that someone was sending Hank Williams songs as murder invitations sooner or later. I wondered who he'd talked to. Flippo? Cleve? Bill Dick? It didn't really matter. What mattered was that given the sensational and competitive nature of the New York press, the public interest in the case and the pressure to solve it were going to skyrocket. This was bad news for the cops. And it was bad news for me. Because it wasn't going to be an easy case to solve. And that was putting it mildly.

It was the first time I'd thought of Hank Williams all day. Of course it was only eleven o'clock.

'What do I do with Joe the Hyena?' I asked Rambam. 'Send him a thank-you note or something?'

'No,' said Rambam, 'you already did your bit for him at the bank when you saved his daughter-in-law.'

I watched the December sunshine splash into the loft and felt it chase away some of the chill. I was starting to feel pretty good. Maybe it was the espresso, or maybe it was the warming thought that I'd saved somebody's life and that people were grateful for it.

'You're lucky,' said Rambam. 'Most guys do their bit at the bank, they only get a toaster.'

24

It was half past Gary Cooper time and I was out buying cat food. The sun was no longer anywhere to be seen. Maybe it thought it would knock off early. Get away before the rush hour. I was halfway to the grocery store when it started to rain. I never run when it starts raining. I just keep to my same leisurely pace and try to walk between the drops. You get about equally wet either way, but if you run you look stupid. If you walk you just look crazy. There's more dignity in crazy, and it's also less strenuous.

As a general concession to the rain, however, I decided to stop at a fancy little gourmet shop. About all they seemed to sell were gourmet pistachio nuts and cat food at ninety-seven cents a can. I bought four cans. They didn't give Green Stamps.

On my way back home in the rain I saw a man with his hand out and a wet cardboard sign around his neck. It said I AM A VET. PLEASE HELP ME. I gave him five bucks. He gave me a salute. I turned the corner and went home.

I fed the cat, lit a cigar, and walked over to the window. I watched the raindrops scamper down the rusty fire escapes across the street. The cat finished eating and she jumped up on the windowsill. We watched the rain together for a long time.

I felt inexpressibly lonely. 'Hey,' I said to the cat. 'I ever tell you about the time in Vietnam . . .'

The cat kept watching the rain.

I called Gunner around dusk.

'Hello,' said a breathless British voice.

'Did I interrupt something?'

'No,' said Gunner, 'I've been in the darkroom all afternoon.'

'Grow mushrooms in there?' I asked.

'No,' she said.

'Didn't think so,' I said. 'Want to join me for dinner at the Derby tomorrow night?'

'Let me check my schedule,' she said. 'Oh. I have a session at six. But I could meet you around nine.'

'Fine,' I said.

'Fine,' she said. The last time I'd taken a broad to dinner on a Saturday night, I was a young cowboy and Broadway was a prairie. I hung up.

I had more than merely a social interest in Gunner. There were a few stray threads I wanted to gather from her Victorian tweeds. I had been gathering stray threads all week, and I was starting to feel like Rapunzel without a sewing machine. If I could've woven together all the threads I'd gathered on this case, it would've made such an unpleasant-looking web that nobody would have wanted to come into my parlor.

Murray Fishkin, the lawyer, was never in his office when I called. I didn't have the resources or the authority to corral

84

a guy like Fishkin, but I was going to have to find some way to get to him pretty fast. Also I planned to get a little tighter with Simmons and Flippo – see if I noticed any veiled threats or new facial tics.

I poured out a shot of Jameson and downed it at my desk. Suspects were only suspects. All you could do was suspect them. When you got right down to it, there was an art to knowing when not to bang your head against the wall. I downed another shot of Jameson. I fished around in the wastebasket and found a decent-looking half-smoked cigar and I fired it up. Gives you a little buzz that a fresh one never quite comes up to.

I would wait. Let the killer make the next move in this chess game. All killers lacked one important quality. They lacked, as Holmes himself put it, 'that supreme gift of the artist – the knowledge of when to stop.'

Hank was bound to strike again. When he did, I planned to catch him and feed him to the iguana. I tossed off another jolt of Jameson. I'd just sit here and wait for something to happen.

Waiting was boring. Most people spend their lives waiting. For trains to pass. For princes to come. For agents to call. For ships to come in. For phone calls that will change their lives. I was no different.

I was waiting for a killer to kill.

25

The Monkey's Paw, full of stifling warmth and hollow laughter, reached out to the lonely denizens of the freezing sidewalk and pulled them inside with a greedy simian fist. A cold rain that had begun earlier in the evening had now turned to sleet. Not the sort of night to be gazing at quaint window displays in quaint little Village shops. It was too damn cold to be quaint.

General Sheridan was still there, of course, holding the fort, with sleet bouncing like enemy bullets off his greatcoat. He was about the only guy who ever hung out in the square who wasn't a degenerate. He looked proud, stern, and disapproving, even with an icicle on his nose. He might have been a mediocre general, but he made a great statue.

I arrived at the Monkey's Paw about a quarter after Cinderella's deadline.

'You're late,' said Ratso. He was tucked into a far corner at the bend of the bar near the radiator.

'You never gave Marilyn Monroe that crap when she was late, Ratso,' I said.

'Those were different times,' said Ratso. 'We were young, restless, carefree, white, liberal . . . stupid.'

'You can say that again,' I said.

'I can't remember it,' said Ratso.

We ordered a round from Tommy the bartender. 'Let's put this one on the *Lampoon*,' I said.

'The rate you're going, you're gonna put it on that ugly hunting vest of yours,' said Ratso.

'Put a sock on it,' I said. 'I'm not scheduled to perform neurosurgery for at least two more hours.'

Tommy brought the drinks. I took a hearty slug of mine. Just to cut the phlegm.

'First of all, Ratso,' I said, 'I want to thank you for helping me the other night.' I knocked off the rest of the shot.

'How?' asked Ratso.

'Remember at the loft we were talking about right-handed and left-handed shadows? I was depressed about how the case was not going anywhere? You said, "Don't be so negative"?'

'Yeah?'

'Well, that's good advice anytime,' I said, 'but it's especially pertinent when you're talking about contact sheets. It's the negative, Ratso. The negative was reversed.' I motioned to Tommy for another round.

'In the picture of me and Reshevsky, the white square is at each player's right hand. The next day, I went to the cop shop and got Cooperman to show me the contact sheet again. Those guys playing chess in Washington Square Park. Remember? The *black* square was at each player's right hand.'

Tommy brought over a Bass ale and a shot of Jameson for me and a vodka grapefruit juice for Ratso. Ratso was under the impression that this drink would help him lose weight. I doubted if it was true, but the more he drank, the skinnier my wallet looked.

'I promise you one thing,' I said. 'When the murderer is caught, he'll be left-handed.'

'Jesus,' said Ratso. 'I thought the killer came from Houston. Obviously a red herring.'

'Obviously,' I said.

Several grapefruit orchards later I told Ratso the nature of the 'clue' I'd seen in 'Settin' the Woods on Fire.' The connection, as it were, between the song and Bubba Borgelt's death.

'This is a sick clue,' I said. 'You didn't see it in the song because you have a normal mind.'

'Maybe normal is too strong a word,' said Ratso.

'Ingenuous, childlike, trusting . . .'

'Yeah,' said Ratso. It was only one word, but he was starting to slur it.

'What I'm going to tell you doesn't bring us much closer to the identity of the killer, but it does give us a good glimpse of his mind at work. An unpleasant spectacle at best.'

'Lay it on me,' said Ratso. 'Maybe I'll empathize.' He laughed a short, nervous laugh. I lit a cigar.

'Don't count on it,' I said. I puffed at the cigar a bit. It wasn't bad.

'Okay,' I said. 'I knew this prison guard once, down in Texas. He was telling me about what an execution was like in the electric chair. He said that they always strapped the doomed men down to the chair much more heavily than you'd think necessary. If they didn't, he said, "they'd get up and dance around."

'Well, that's what happened Monday night to Bubba Borgelt. Except nobody strapped him down.'

'What do you mean?' Ratso asked.

'I mean somebody wanted Bubba to dance. Somebody who looks at life through the eyes of evil.

'The killer, I imagine, rather fancied the little bridge in the song:

> 'We'll take in all the honky-tonks.
> Tonight we're havin' fun.
> We'll show the folks a brand new dance
> That never has been done.

'The killer made those lines come to life in a way Hank Williams never dreamed of. He saw perverse possibilities in that old tune that would only occur to an extremely sick cowboy. We saw the "brand new dance" on Monday night on the stage of the Lone Star. The killer employed Borgelt's body and his soul. To show the folks. To bring that spine-snapping, heart-stopping, hypnotizing, horribly out-of-control breakdance to the stage for one night only. Somebody planned it, chuckled over it to himself, carried it out without a hitch, and watched the whole hideous performance right there with the rest of us. An attractive picture, isn't it?'

Ratso sat silent for a long moment. He shook his head slowly, like he was trying to shake off a memory that you can't shake off. He tried a little laugh, but it didn't take. Ratso looked at me. I looked at Ratso.

'Shocking, Sherlock,' he said.

26

My kitchen table looked like Lou Grant's desk on a bad day. It was littered with almost the whole week's newspapers, and they weren't there so I could follow octopus beak futures. I needed all the information I could get on the 'Lone Star Killer' and the 'Hank Williams Murders,' as he and they had now come to be known.

I moved sluggishly into my second cup of espresso and lit a cigar. I looked at the front page of Tuesday's *Daily News*. The headline was PLUCK SECOND STRINGER AT LONE STAR. I settled back in my chair and searched through the pile until I found a typically amazing headline on a late edition of Thursday's *New York Post*. The article was obviously written when very little new information was coming in on the story. The *Post* headline read SECOND STAR SLAIN – LINKED TO MAYOR.

I sipped a little more espresso and puffed at the cigar. The *Times* had been a trifle late with the news, but by Wednesday it had acknowledged that indeed something out of the ordinary was occurring at the Lone Star Cafe. By Friday it had jumped aboard with both feet and was attempting to lead the way again. The headline on the story in Friday's *New York Times* was IS IT TIME TO BAN COUNTRY MUSIC?

The stories were all remarkably similar. There were interviews with Lone Star owner Bill Dick in which I learned the size of his boat – forty-two feet – and several other things about it I hadn't wanted to know, and with the Lone Star manager, my old pal Cleve, who seemed to have become an expert on criminology, electrical wiring, educating the public, and psychology in general. I'd always thought he was just a road musician who drifted into the job when his band had decided to disband.

The other name that kept popping up in the stories was that of Chet Flippo. He was a bona fide Hank Williams expert, and as such he was suddenly in great demand. 'Why did the killer resort to such an odd method of communicating his death threats?' asked the reporter. 'As I point out in my book . . . ,' responded Flippo. And so forth.

Questions were also put to Fox and Cooperman, as they appeared to be the most prominent NYPD operatives on the case. 'We have no suspects at the moment.' 'We are following several leads right now.' 'We're working on it.' Things didn't look real promising.

Everybody wanted to know what was really going on. Nobody really knew except one person. And he wasn't talking.

The phones rang. I got up, made it over to the desk, and nabbed the one on the left on the second ring. A few more rings might've cauterized my brain. It was 3.04 p.m. It was Chet Flippo.

'Hi there,' he said. 'I'm calling to invite you to a literary event. Tomorrow afternoon between three and six at the Lone Star. It's a party for the book.'

'Sounds like a lot of fun,' I said.

'It's interesting,' said Flippo. 'Ever been to one of these literary affairs?'

'No,' I said.

'You really ought to come then,' he said.

'I went to a cock fight once in Mexico,' I said. Flippo laughed a hearty literary laugh.

'See you tomorrow,' he said.

I hung up and looked at the unopened book still sitting where I'd left it on the corner of the desk. Maybe I'd have to read the damn thing. Could a book on the life of a country singer who died thirty-three years ago shed any light on the menace of a modern-day killer who was stalking New York City? Impossible, I thought.

Highly improbable, anyway.

Nine-thirty, Saturday night. I was sitting at the little bar in the Derby on MacDougal Street, working on my third Courvoisier and waiting for Gunner. I never used to like Courvoisier but I knew somebody once who used to love it, and I used to love her. So now I drank Courvoisier sometimes and smiled to myself. If somebody was watching me drinking alone there, and smiling to myself, they might've thought I was plotting to kill my wife. But I wasn't. I didn't have a wife.

'Hello,' said a voice behind me. I turned in time to catch a dazzler of a smile. 'Did I keep you waiting long?' she asked.

'Yeah,' I said. I employed an economy of words. Women go for the strong, silent type. Except in rare cases where they prefer the highly verbal, indecisive type. I could be either. Sometimes, in extreme situations, I would rapidly alternate the two personas in case the woman liked a guy who was confused about his identity. I didn't work at it too hard, though. I didn't really give a damn what a woman thought. That was probably the reason my personal life was a shipwreck. I treated women like everybody else, and no matter what they may tell you, that ain't the ticket. Usually.

'This is a cute place,' said Gunner.

'Yeah,' I said.

'Yeah?' she asked. 'Yeah. That's all you say to anybody? Yeah?'

'Yeah,' I said.

She sat down next to me at the bar. She put her hand on my shoulder.

'I think you say "yeah" because you want people to think you're a tough guy,' she said softly but distinctly. She was looking me right in the eyes. She wouldn't take her hand off my shoulder. I didn't mind too much. It was her hand. She could put it anywhere she wanted. 'You're not really a tough guy, are you?' she asked.

'Not really,' I said. I killed the last of the Courvoisier. 'I just like to say "yeah" a lot. It's part of a Beatle lyric I heard once. You hungry?'

'I'm starved,' she said.

'Good,' I said. 'We'll order a couple of big, hairy steaks.'

'Sounds charming,' she said.

We took a table in the back, had some wine. I let Gunner pick the wine. Always let the woman choose the wine. Makes you look sensitive, innocent. Maybe a little vulnerable. It's also usually cheaper because the woman is trying to protect you because she thinks you're so vulnerable.

Gunner ordered a very expensive bottle of French wine. I couldn't speak enough frog to even read the label. As the waiter was opening the bottle, Gunner said to me, 'Ever try this before?'

'No,' I said, 'I usually stick with Château de Cat Piss.' She looked pretty as a picture as she laughed a little light British laugh. Just to pass the time until the guy pulled the cork. As I looked at her, she began to look even prettier than a picture. Prettier than any picture she was ever likely to take.

A fleeting thought crossed a dusty desk in my mind. Not so much a thought, maybe, as a feeling. I didn't like the feeling. It was a sort of irrational confusion heavily laced with distrust. Distrust for the vision sitting across the table from me.

What did I really know about this broad? Not a bloody lot. She looked too beautiful to be trusted. Too good to be true. I didn't even know for sure that the photos she showed us at Costello's were taken when she said they'd been. Or if she'd tampered with them first. Certainly not. But she did seem to have an uncanny knack of being nearby scenes of mysterious death. So what? I had that same little knack myself. Had Gunner left the Lone Star before somebody'd turned on the juice and cut Bubba loose? She'd stayed the whole damn night. Why leave just before the last song?

Was I just being paranoid? Probably. But if you're paranoid long enough, sooner or later you're gonna be right. The waiter was struggling with the cork and I was struggling with the notion that Gunner was holding back. That she knew something that I needed to know. But I didn't know what I needed to know that she knew. If that made any sense. I smiled at her across the table. She smiled back. What the hell. You had to trust somebody.

'I hope it's a good year,' said Gunner.

'So far it's been a pretty lousy one,' I said. 'I don't know about you, but for me the year started fairly slowly. After a while it picked up a little steam, and life became merely tedious. Then, just when it was looking like the worm of happiness was beginning to turn my way, this little spot of bother arises at the Lone Star and throws my whole goddamn life into a hideous, murderous snarl. I don't know. . . . Maybe next year will be better. Who knows?' I gave Gunner my careless, hopeful, survivor's smile.

She smiled back. A brief, rather patronizing smile. 'I was talking about the wine,' she said.

27

On balance, the evening had been a success. That's what I thought as I rode up to my loft in the freight elevator with the one exposed light bulb. There is very little you can do with a freight elevator. You can't very well hang a Tiffany lampshade in it. That would be gauche.

The Hank Williams Killer was far away, I thought. You had to think of something when you rode in a freight elevator or you might as well be freight.

Inside the loft, I patted the cat and checked for any messages on the answering machine. Nobody loved me.

I put on my sarong, killed the light, and went to sleep concentrating on not dreaming about miniature babies.

The phone rang by my bedside. I hit the light and looked at the clock. It was crowding three o'clock in the morning. I was one of those guys that didn't mind getting woke up in the middle of the night. Probably should've been a fireman or a country doctor. I didn't have a wife. Didn't have any kids. Didn't have a job to go to in the morning. Didn't go to church. Didn't give a damn if somebody called me in the middle of the night.

Just as long as I didn't pick up the phone and find it was me on the other end of the line. I picked up the phone. It wasn't me.

It was Gunner.

'Somebody's broken into my apartment,' she said.

Her lost-little-girl inflection combined with the British accent made her sound like one of the three bears saying, 'Somebody's been sleeping in my bed.' Unfortunately, I wasn't the guilty party.

'You all right?' I asked. 'You call the cops?'

'Yes,' she said wearily. 'They've been and gone. I'm all in, I'll tell you.'

'Anything missing?' I asked.

'What do you think is missing?' she fairly shouted.

'No idea,' I said. 'Something's missing from every life, they say.'

'Well, something's sure missing from mine,' she said. 'And I'm scared.' She sounded close to tears.

'Tell me,' I said in a softer tone.

'What's missing from mine . . . is every print, contact, and negative of everything I've ever shot at the Lone Star Cafe.'

28

'Where's your friend Gunner?' asked Cleve with a fairly satanic leer. The Lone Star was humming with activity. People and books and bottles of beer were everywhere you looked and a few places you didn't. Hank Williams music was blaring out of the house speakers and Lone Star Five-Alarm Chili was coming down the line as fast as Fong, the Chinese cook, could slop it into the bowls. Quite a literary event.

'Who's Gunner?' asked Downtown Judy petulantly as soon as Cleve strolled away. I wasn't sure I knew myself.

'Oh, Gunner's a photographer person I've been doing some work with,' I said. Sadly, this was true. 'Never above you, never below you, always by your side' was about as far as I'd got.

'Is Gunner a man or a woman?' asked Downtown Judy. She wasn't one to beat around the bush, especially if she thought the situation threatened her bush.

'Is who a man or a woman?' asked Ratso as he scurried up, balancing a bottle of Lone Star, a bowl of chili, and a book.

'Gunner,' said Downtown Judy.

'She's a broad Kinky's currently hosing. She's a fucking gorgeous broad,' Ratso laughed. Downtown Judy looked at me.

'She's not that gorgeous,' I said. I tried to give Ratso a disparaging look, but he was busy eating his chili.

'Have I ever met her?' asked Judy.

'No,' I said. 'I've hardly met her myself.'

Ratso looked up from his chili and winked at me conspiratorially. He was laughing so hard he couldn't eat. 'Pretty good chili,' he said.

Downtown Judy turned away from him and gazed into my eyes. She looked like a little puppy dog that might suddenly grow up to be the Hound of the Baskervilles. And if she did, I doubted if she'd know 'c'mere' from 'sic 'em.'

'I didn't think you liked the chili here, Ratso,' I said.

'It's the only thing on the menu today,' he said. 'Lone Star beer and chili. Very trendy.'

'It's chic, all right,' I said. 'I've got to find Bill Dick. I'll be back.'

I navigated my way through the crowd on the stairs and fought my way to the bar on the second floor. I didn't see anybody I knew except the bartender. Most of the people I knew were probably still sleeping off Saturday night.

I pointed to a guy standing next to me who was holding a beer bottle. The bartender got me a beer.

I looked around at the ponderous little groups of people all over the place and went out the door and on to the rear staircase. It was cooler and quieter, and no literary lions were there. I sat down on the stairs and sipped the beer. I gathered my thoughts.

I didn't have a mother-in-law. That was one of the advantages of not being married. And yet something had been nagging me all morning. Relentlessly. If it had only been a mother-in-law it wouldn't have been such a problem. I could've just called Joe the Hyena and had her legs broken. Had her left in the trunk of a Budget Rent-A-Car out at JFK.

But what was nagging me had nothing to do with the mother-in-law I didn't have. And it was very serious and very real. It had to do with Gunner.

Seven days had passed since Bubba Borgelt had been braised. The killer appeared to strike viciously, and then go into hibernation for a while, leaving no tracks. Except those he wanted us to follow. Why?

'Hey, man,' said a familiar voice from under a cowboy hat. 'How's the murder investigation comin'?' It was Lee, the other manager of the place besides Cleve. He looked like a black Tom Mix. His wife, Leni, ran the cloakroom setup. She was a doll.

'It's coming about as good as your chances of being elected Head Lizard of the White Supremacist Party,' I said. I finished the beer. I put the bottle on the stairs.

'Don't leave it there,' said Lee. 'Somebody come along and trip on it and break their fool neck.'

'Yeah,' I said, 'that on top of two murders could be bad for business.' Lee smiled.

'You kiddin', man?' he asked. 'You have any idea what the ring was last night?' I didn't even know what the ring was any night.

'What's the ring?' I asked.

'The ring,' said Lee impatiently, 'is the cash register. The amount of business at the bar. Last night was the biggest in the whole history of the club. Why you think everybody's buying this guy's book? Everybody wants to see the murder scene for themselves. Everybody's waiting for the Hank Williams Killer to hit again.'

It was a little surprising what people would do. Only a little surprising.

'That's where it's at,' said Lee, and he walked up the stairs. I thought it might be time I looked for Bill Dick.

He'd either be in his office or on his boat, and I hadn't brought my periscope so I thought I'd check his office first.

I saw Ratso and Downtown Judy across the balcony, waved, and headed quickly down the stairs to the first floor. At the foot of the stairs a large, polite mob had gathered around the glowing figure of Chet Flippo. He was talking, signing books, and doing a fair imitation of being gracious. Flippo didn't see me. He was looking through the whole scene. There was something in his eyes I hadn't seen before. I liked it even less than what I'd seen the last time.

Hank's lonely wail came through the speakers, but his words went unnoticed in the din of the sophisticated, glittering crowd. The song went:

> 'Tonight down here in the valley
> I'm lonesome and oh how I feel
> As I sit here alone in my cabin
> I can see your mansion on the hill.'

As I made my way over to the stairs that led down to Bill Dick's office, I also overheard a few phrases from the crowd around Flippo.

'Marvelous economy of words,' one said.

'The characters leap right off the page,' said another.

29

'What a city!' said Bill Dick as he poured us both a glass of something from the decanter on his desk. 'What a city!'

I nodded and took a sip. 'It's not bad,' I said.

'You're damn right it's not bad. I don't care what anybody says about it. New York has rallied around the Lone Star.'

'I was talking about the drink,' I said. 'Drink's not bad. City's rotten.' I took another sip.

'Think what you want,' said Bill Dick, 'but the people of New York have come through for the Lone Star.' I thought of that woman who was stabbed about eighty-seven times and screamed for help for nearly an hour before she died. More than a hundred people had heard her. Nobody'd called the cops. Nobody'd helped. Kitty something, her name was, I thought, though it didn't make a hell of a lot of difference now. The same sort of ghouls who let her die were now thronging to the Lone Star Cafe.

Bill poured me another drink. I didn't say anything. Bill looked at me. 'Right or wrong, Kinkster?' he asked.

My mind was still trying to think of Kitty's last name, but it was drawing a blank. 'Right, Bill,' I said.

'Life goes on, Kinkster. There's still a business that some-body's got to run. There's still a lot of problems to deal with.'

'I can imagine,' I said. 'If you don't mind my asking, what are the problems? Aside from the two obvious ones. Two stiffs that used to be stars.'

'They're still stars, Kinkster,' said Bill Dick.

'Tell that to Gabby Hayes,' I said. Bill shifted uncomfortably in his chair.

'Drawing crowds is no problem now,' he said. 'The problem is getting anybody to play the goddamn club.'

'Can't understand it,' I said.

He smiled a small, brief smile. If he'd held it a little longer you could've called it a wince. 'So we're using house bands temporarily. Cleve's fronting one group. Used to have his own band, you know. Mike Simmons is booked to play a few nights. We'll get by for now, but I don't know how long we can stretch it before we'll have to get a name act in here. Pretty damn quick, I'd say. These crowds can be fickle.'

'And that's a nice word for them,' I said. 'What other problems are you having?' I was having a problem believing anybody'd play the place again. Of course, when you needed a gig, you needed a gig.

'The other problems we can handle,' he said. 'Petty theft. A case of Jack Daniel's disappears. Somebody's swiped a picture from out of the manager's office. Bartenders robbing you blind. The day-to-day crap that drives you nuts.'

I stood up to go. I had problems of my own. 'I've got to get upstairs,' I said. 'Before I go, though, I'd like you to explain something to me. I don't need the details. Just nut-shell it for me. Could anybody have rigged that electrical system to french-fry Bubba Borgelt?'

If I'd wanted a one-word answer, it would've been pretty disappointing. I was glad I didn't have a train to catch.

'I know a good bit about electrical wiring,' he said. 'Now the guitar amp wasn't grounded. It was sitting at a potential of a hundred twenty volts AC.' At this point Dick resorted to drawing little diagrams on his desk. I didn't ask any questions. I didn't know what the hell he was talking about.

'Hey,' I said, 'I'm not the Wichita lineman. Put the thing in layman's terms.'

'Anybody could have done it,' he said. 'Borgelt's body completed the circuit. With that sweaty, salt-drenched outfit, by the end of the last set he was a perfect human conductor.' There was an eagerness flashing in Dick's eyes. They appeared faintly electrical and almost happy. I thanked him for his help and went upstairs.

Things had thinned out a hair. Now you could cross the room without having to turn sideways. I joined Ratso at the downstairs bar. Simmons was hanging on to him like a fungus growing out of his left elbow. We all had a drink.

'Doubles for everybody, bartender,' said Simmons. 'Rocks.'

'What was that woman's name,' I asked, 'that was being stabbed to death and you know, was screaming forever, and a hundred people heard her and didn't do anything?'

'Oh, yeah,' said Ratso, 'I remember – Kitty . . . uh, Kitty – '

'Kitty what?' I asked impatiently. The bartender brought the drinks.

'Kitty . . .' said Simmons. 'Kitty . . . I know it . . . it's right on the tip of my knife.'

Downtown Judy walked up behind us. She'd taken a cigarette out of her purse and was waiting for somebody to light it.

'Kitty Genovese!' I shouted.

'You're good with names,' said Ratso.

'Who's Kitty Genovese?' asked Downtown Judy.

We gravitated, if that was the word, to the upstairs bar. It was closing in on five o'clock, but it seemed like we'd spent several incarnations at the Lone Star. Einstein's theory applied. Time was relative, and time spent at literary affairs was relatively tedious.

We'd lost Simmons, but picked up Cleve and Flippo. I figured I'd play like Jack Webb and ask Cleve a few routine questions. I wasn't in much shape to ask hard ones. I'd let Downtown Judy ask the hard ones.

'So Cleve,' I said, 'what's the security like down there in the manager's office? What about this picture that's missing?'

'Obviously, you've talked to Bill,' said Cleve. 'Christ, I wish he'd get off my back about all this shit. Of course, security down there is nonexistent. What the hell does he expect?'

'What about this picture?' I asked.

'Yeah, that is a strange one,' he said. 'The damn thing materialized out of nowhere one morning – nobody knows where it came from – then, just when Bill tells me to have it framed, it disappears.' Maybe I was imagining things, but it seemed like Flippo, sitting down the bar from us, was becoming increasingly engrossed in our conversation.

'Well,' I said, 'what's the big deal? Was this a valuable goddamn painting?' I thought of Gauguin's last letter, in which he stated, 'I have been defeated by poverty.' The letter is now owned by David Rockefeller. Why not? Flippo was definitely listening now.

'No,' said Cleve. 'It was hardly a case of where did Vincent Van Gogh?' He laughed a little. I didn't. 'It wasn't a goddamn oil painting or anything. It was just an old photo. But it was autographed. The picture was autographed, so I guess that made it valuable. I don't know.'

'Who was the picture of?' I asked. Flippo was looking away. A bit too unconcerned suddenly.

'Christ,' said Cleve. 'Didn't Dick tell you?'

'Apparently he didn't or I wouldn't be asking you,' I said.

'It was a picture of Hank Williams,' said Cleve.

30

Monday morning I was working on my first cup of espresso and looking over a little stiff chart I'd written down on a Big Chief tablet. It had been two and a half weeks since Larry Barkin had gone to Jesus. It was exactly a week since Bubba Borgelt's rather unpleasant demise. During this time Bill Dick had been able to coax only three name acts into playing the club: Jerry Jeff Walker, Asleep at the Wheel, and the Burrito Brothers. Nothing out of line had occurred on those three occasions. I considered this with a troubled spirit. Why had Hank picked on Barkin and Borgelt and let Walker, Asleep at the Wheel, and the Burritos pass by unscathed?

According to reports from Cleve and Ratso, the crowds of the curious were still coming like morbid moths to the doily of death that hung over the place. This continued to make the cash register register.

In fact, for Bill Dick, murder, unpleasant and un-American as it was, was beginning to look like a financial pleasure.

I moved thoughtfully into my second cup of espresso. I lit my first cigar of the morning and leaned back in the chair by my desk. A number of patterns were beginning to come together fairly clearly in my cranium. I wasn't a rocket scientist, but there were occasions when I was able to put two and two together and come up with something moderately wiggy.

I thought of the Hank Williams picture that Cleve had said was missing from the Lone Star. Then I remembered a snatch of conversation in which someone had told me, 'He let me take a photograph.' My reasoning went like this: *Gonif* is the Yiddish word for 'thief.' *Gonif* is Yiddish. Gunner is British. Therefore Gunner is a *gonif*.

I called Gunner.

It was not a particularly pleasant phone call, but it confirmed what I'd suspected. Gunner had lifted the photograph from the Lone Star. She had, in the words of Jesse Winchester, been 'taken by a photograph' she'd seen on a desk in the manager's office. It was a photo of a 'tall, gaunt man in a big white cowboy hat standing with two small boys by a sign that said HOWIE'S #1 BBQ. A contrasty print,' she'd said. 'A grainy texture. A large sky. A fifties feel to it.'

Translated from the argot of the trendy fashion photographer, that meant she liked the picture.

'So where's the photo now?' I asked.

'That's just it,' she said. 'I've looked everywhere. It might have been taken along with everything else when my place was broken into. I never even got a chance to take it out of the envelope I'd put it in.'

'Terrific,' I said. 'Do you remember anything about the picture? This is important now, Gunner.' It was more important than even I knew at the time.

'This – this didn't have anything to do with what's been happening at the Lone Star, did it?' she asked with a rising note of anxiety.

'No, of course not,' I said. No point in upsetting her further. It was bad enough to be known as a *gonif*. 'Tell me about the picture,' I said.

'I told you about the picture,' she said. 'HOWIE'S #1 BBQ. The man with the white hat, the small boys in cowboy suits. Did I mention that? They were dressed in cute little matching cowboy outfits?'

'No,' I said.

'Standing one on each side of him by the roadside. And there was some writing, maybe a signature and a date somewhere on the bottom.'

'You don't remember the signature? The date?'

'I don't recall the signature,' she said, 'but the date was December 31, 1952. It's my mum's birthday so I remembered it. I only saw the bloody thing for a few seconds when it was on the desk.' Amazing, the things people remembered in life. Even I remembered a few things. The way Gunner'd looked sitting across from me at the Derby.

'Large sky, contrasty print, fifties feel – anything else?' I asked.

'You're poking fun at me now,' she laughed nervously.

'You know who that was a photograph of?' I asked.

'No,' she said, 'but he had the saddest eyes I've ever seen. I can still see his eyes. Who was he?'

'Hank Williams,' I said.

'Oh, God,' she said. I could hear the dread in her voice.

She didn't know what Hank looked like, but she'd certainly read the papers. She knew about the Hank Williams Killer. She'd been close to the scene of two of his 'performances.' 'Shit,' she said in a little, frightened voice, 'you've got to be joking.'

'I wish I was,' I said.

Monday night I was watching *Monday Night Football* like any other good American. I had a black-and-white television set that an old dope dealer had given to me. You needed a screwdriver to adjust the volume, and you needed pliers to change the channel. The set probably would've worked better if you'd just chopped it up and snorted it.

Sometime during the third quarter the phone rang. It was Ratso.

'Hold the weddin',' I said. I put down the blower, got the screwdriver and turned off the set, found a half-smoked cigar in the wastebasket, fired it up, and picked up the blower again.

'Start talkin',' I said.

'Murray Fishkin,' said Ratso. 'Was that his name?'

'That *is* his name,' I said.

'*Was* his name,' said Ratso. 'He took a brody yesterday. It's right here in the paper.'

I puffed on my cigar. So the bald-headed lawyer had iced himself. I'd never even met the man, so I wasn't greatly grieved at his final passing of the bar.

'What does it mean?' Ratso asked.

'It means he'll be out of his office even more now,' I said. 'It means he's no longer a serious suspect, unless the murders suddenly stop. I don't think they will.'

'Jesus,' said Ratso.

'It also means,' I said, 'that the killer is almost certainly a close, personal friend of mine.'

'You're kidding,' said Ratso.

'Present company excluded, of course,' I said.

31

It was Thursday night. Six shopping days until Christmas, and I still didn't know what I wanted out of life. I hadn't made a shopping list of things for anybody else either. You give what you get.

I'd been keeping in almost daily touch with Ratso and Cleve concerning the case and any new developments at the Lone Star. No new songs had arrived. Not many singers, either.

The holidays are a slow time for most occupational groups. It's not much different with country singers-turned-amateur detectives. So when I'd finished rearranging my sock drawer, I picked up Flippo's book on Hank Williams. I'd been languidly plowing through it for some time actually. Unfortunately, I'd only gotten about as far as Flippo's autograph.

I didn't much like reading biographies. Real life was tedious enough. I didn't want to read about dead country singers. I'd been to that rodeo.

I camped in the loft for several days. I survived by heating up Bill Dick's frozen Five-Alarm Chili, drinking espresso, and smoking cigars. The Beverly Hills Diet.

Everywhere I looked I saw Hank's mournful eyes.

I read.

I also organized an extensive, far-reaching telephone operation like a Mafia don in prison. When I wasn't on the phone, I was reading Flippo's book. When I wasn't reading Flippo's book, I was on the phone. I began to gently probe the backgrounds of some of my 'friends.'

The only other media input I allowed myself was

watching *Quincy* reruns. I had begun to regard Quincy as a close, personal friend. Not really a healthy situation, interpersonally speaking.

The book stayed with me like a bottle imp or an albatross. I read on.

Hank Williams' horse was named Hi-life. Hank's first wife was named Audrey. His second wife, Billie Jean, married country singer Johnny Horton after Hank's death. Horton also died tragically young.

It was almost two o'clock in the morning when I learned that the name Hank Williams had used when he checked into hotels was Herman P. Willis.

It was a pretty obscure piece of information. Even a knowledgeable, veteran soul like myself hadn't known about it.

I read like a demon in the night. Hank's brief, troubled life flashed through my consciousness like the meteor that it was. Lawsuits, divorce, rhinestones, guns, drugs, alcohol, pain, loneliness, untimely death.

Have a nice day.

According to Flippo's book, there was the time on the road that Hank was arrested for taking a shot at a picture of the battleship *Missouri* hanging on a wall in a restaurant. He told the arresting officers: 'It drew on me first.'

There was the night of June 11, 1949, when Hank electrified the Grand Ol' Opry for the first time, receiving more encores than any other performer before or since. There was the time he sold one of his songs to Little Jimmy Dickens for two bottles of Southern Comfort, and the time he bought the lyrics to 'Cold, Cold Heart' from Paul Gilley.

There was the lifelong struggle between Hank's mother, Lilly, and Hank's wife Audrey for his money and his soul, roughly in that order. It was a lifelong struggle that did not stop at Hank's death. Very little stopped at Hank's death, except, of course, ol' Hank. He and Herman P. Willis were buried in Montgomery in the same grave. Hank's music and fame continued to live and grow, but Herman P. Willis was forgotten. Or almost forgotten.

Then there was the famous show on a cold winter's day in January 1953, in Canton, Ohio. The show that Hank never played. Hank's chauffeur-driven Cadillac had rolled like a death train through four southern states, through countless towns, through the morphine-hazed, broken-hearted, perpetual night that had become his life. From Montgomery to Chattanooga, where Hank stopped at a diner and tipped a waiter fifty dollars, to Knoxville, where he received several mysterious shots from an equally mysterious doctor. In Rutledge, Tennessee, a cop stopped the Cadillac for speeding. The cop looked at the figure slumped in the back and said, 'Hey, that guy looks dead.' The chauffeur explained that Hank was only sedated.

The Cadillac rolled through Bristol, Cedarville, Chilhowie, Marion, Wytheville, Bluefield, where Hank again stopped to see a doctor, and Princeton, West Virginia, where he stopped at a bar, Beckley, Willis Branch and Oak Hill, where Charles Carr, the chauffeur, finally checked the back seat and realized that Hank Williams was as cold as the lonely highway in the winter night.

'Patrolman Jamey drove the Cadillac to the Oak Hill Hospital,' said Flippo's book, 'where Hank Williams was a Dead on Arrival. There had been another man in the car with Hank and Charles Carr. He told Jamey that his name was Donald Surface and that he was a relief driver that Carr had picked up in Bluefield, West Virginia. Donald Surface then vanished.'

After the biggest funeral the South had ever seen, both of Hank's devoted wives organized country bands and hit the road, each billing herself as 'Mrs Hank Williams.' A touching tribute.

By the time I'd finished the book it was almost dawn.

I rubbed my eyes and thought about the pages I'd read. It was the first book I'd cracked in years that wasn't a murder mystery. I smiled at the ironic notion that reading it might very possibly help solve a real-life murder mystery.

I could see the sun just barely etching the warehouses to the east, like a light over the top of a doorway. The morning wasn't the only thing dawning on me. But it was a hell of a lot more attractive.

As it turned out, I'd finished reading Flippo's book barely in time to save my life.

32

Tompall and the Glaser Brothers played the Lone Star Cafe that Sunday night. Tompall had been sort of my country music godfather when I was in Nashville, and Chuck Glaser had produced my first album, *Sold American*, in 1973. The other two brothers, Jim and Ned, I had met only a few times. Tompall and the Glaser Brothers were considered by many, myself included, to be the finest vocal group ever to hit Nashville.

I went to the show with Rambam. I watched the show while Rambam cased the club for a place of concealment when they closed for the night. Hank had not sent a song to the Glaser Brothers. In fact he hadn't been heard from in several weeks. He was overdue.

That's why, when I finally said good night to the Glasers at two o'clock in the morning in their dressing room, I was pleased to notice Rambam climbing stealthily into the belly of the iguana.

In the cab home I thought about things. I'd seen almost

everyone connected with the case during the course of the evening. In my mind I went over the lot. Ratso, Cleve, Bill Dick, Chet Flippo, Mike Simmons. Also there'd been Cooperman, Fox, McGovern, Mick Brennan, and many other journalists and photographers I knew on sight. If they'd been hoping for a story, they hadn't gotten one.

The only person I'd expected to see and didn't was Gunner.

Things at the club had been pretty edgy all night. There was almost palpable relief when the show was over and everything was all right. I was feeling pretty relieved too.

When I got back to the loft, I poured a few shots into the bull's horn and finished 'em off. I'd taken my boots off and was sitting at the desk talking to the cat when the phones rang. I picked up the blower on the left.

'Dr Kinky at your cervix,' I said. I'd sort of being expecting a call from one of the Judys.

It wasn't one of the Judys. It was Sergeant Cooperman, and he was not amused.

And everything wasn't all right.

'What seems to be the problem, Officer?' I asked.

'Another bumpkin got waxed tonight, Tex,' said Cooperman in a tired, offhanded manner.

'Jesus,' I said.

'Yeah,' said Cooperman, 'that's what eight million New Yorkers are going to say tomorrow when they wake up and read the newspapers. Was a guy named Ned Glaser. Played the Lone Star last night. He's the brother of Tompall Glaser, who's a friend of yours I believe, so I thought you might want to know. We found him a couple of hours ago out on the West Side Highway where the construction work just sort of stops where the city ran out of funds. You know, just some columns and girders and shit. It goes nowhere. Like this case. Found him behind the wheel of a stolen eighty-two Buick fucking Skylark with a screwdriver in his back. You with me?'

"Fraid so,' I said. I lit a cigar with a surprisingly steady hand. I was a little surprised. Just a little surprised. 'Find anything else?' I asked.

'Yeah. A bottle of wine and a deck of cards. No prints on either of them. No prints on the screwdriver. You get any bright ideas, give us a call.'

'Okay,' I said.

'Adiós,' said Cooperman.

Two hours later the second call came in. I was in bed but I wasn't asleep yet. I was counting screwdrivers.

'Rambam here,' said Rambam, 'of the Village Irregulars. I'm at the pay phone in the doorway of Sarge's Delicatessen watching forty hookers eat dill pickles.'

'Maybe there're keeping in practice,' I said.

I could hear a cash register up close and a siren in the background. Those two sounds, I thought, pretty well covered the spiritual waterfront as far as New York went. And that was far enough for anybody.

'How do you know they're hookers?' I asked.

'Because they look like hookers,' said Rambam. 'Who the hell else would be at Sarge's Delicatessen at five o'clock in the morning eating dill pickles?' There was a pause and I heard the receiver bang against the wall a few times, and then I heard Rambam's daggerlike voice stabbing the New York night.

'Excuse me, miss, are you a hooker?' he asked. I heard a chair scrape and a woman start to say something, but I missed her response. Then Rambam was back. 'I know a hooker when I see one. By the way, I got what you wanted,' he said. 'It says "Tompall and the Glaser Brothers." Big block letters.'

I'd asked him to check out the Lone Star after closing

hours and see what he could see. I especially wanted him to see if he could find a large manila envelope with block letters stashed somewhere in the basement offices. Apparently he had.

'You open it yet?' I asked.

'No,' he said, 'I thought we might share the experience.'

'Is the envelope postmarked?' I asked.

'I don't see one. No. Want me to bring it over?'

'I already know what's in there,' I said.

'If you do you're a fucking Houdini,' said Rambam. 'I haven't opened it yet.'

'It's the Hank Williams song "Lost Highway",' I said.

'All right,' he said, 'let's see. And now, the envelope.' There was a momentary pause, then he came back on the line. 'A fucking Houdini,' he said.

'It's nothing once you know the ropes,' I said. Rambam began reading the contents of the envelope.

'Lost Highway, by Hank Williams,' he intoned.

> 'Just a deck of cards and a jug of wine
> And a woman's lies makes a life like mine.
> Oh, the day we met I went astray
> I started rollin' down that Lost Highway.'

'Nice recitation,' I said.

'Thanks,' said Rambam. 'Shall I keep this for you?'

'Yeah,' I said. 'We can't turn it over to the cops because of how we obtained it. I use the word 'we' loosely. But it is evidence.'

'Evidence of what?' asked Rambam.

'In the words of Sergeant Cooperman, "Another bumpkin got waxed tonight," ' I said. I puffed coolly on what was left of cigar number seven. Rambam didn't say anything.

'A little less enthusiasm, please,' I said. 'Before we

terminate this call, Rambam, tell me exactly where you found that envelope.'

'Can't you guess?' asked Rambam.

'This is getting major-league tedious,' I said.

'Wait a minute,' said Rambam, 'let me get a pickle.' I heard the receiver bang against the wall again a couple of times. Then Rambam came back on the line doing a pretty fair impersonation of a guy eating a pickle on a telephone at five o'clock in the morning. Boy had talent.

'Give up?' he asked.

'Yeah,' I said.

'Want to know where I found it?'

'Yeah,' I said wearily.

'Bottom drawer. Right-hand side of – '

'Goddammit, Rambam,' I said, 'get to the meat of it.'

' – Bill Dick's desk,' he said.

33

Monday afternoon Bill Dick made me an offer I couldn't understand. For some reason he wanted me to play the club. As near as I can recall the conversation ran like this:

'We want you to play the club,' said Bill Dick. 'You name your price.'

'Money may buy me a fine dog,' I said with some dignity, 'but only love can make it wag its tail.' I watched cigar smoke drift up toward the ceiling. What the hell did they want me for? I was too middle-aged to die.

'How about we try to wag its fucking tail five thousand dollars worth?' asked Bill Dick.

'I'm pretty busy,' I said. Actually, I had enough spare time to macramé my nose hairs, but it's never a good idea to let people in New York think you're not busy.

'Busy,' snorted Bill Dick.

'Yeah,' I said. 'I'm workin' on a tampon jingle.'

'We need to overcome this idea,' he continued, 'that the place is jinxed or cursed. You wouldn't believe the shitstorm the media has made out of this. Boyd Matson was down here last night doing a piece for the *Today* show.

'And that was before the Glaser kid was murdered on the West Side. Anything can happen in New York. Right or wrong, Kinkster?'

'Right, Bill,' I said.

'Had nothing to do with his playing the club probably, but you know how people's minds work.'

'Yeah,' I said, 'they think they see a connection.'

'Exactly,' said Bill Dick. 'You're the perfect guy to make New York City safe for country music.'

'Right, Bill,' I said.

'Bubba Borgelt's death was a freak electrical situation. I know electrical wiring inside and out, and when you're working off a high-voltage system and your terminals . . .'

I took the receiver away from my ear and blew a peaceful stream of cigar smoke in the general direction of F. Scott Fitzgerald's letter to his little daughter at camp. It had hung framed on the wall of the loft for as long as I could remember. In the letter, F. Scott had advised his daughter not to worry about the following things: popular opinion, dolls, the past, the future, growing up, anybody getting ahead of you, triumph, failure unless it came through your own fault, mosquitoes, flies, insects in general, parents, boys, disappointments, pleasures and satisfactions. The things to worry about, he'd said, were courage, cleanliness, efficiency, and horsemanship.

Not bad advice in a pinch.

I put the receiver back to my ear and heard Bill Dick say the words 'electrical component.'

I didn't say anything.

'What kind of flowers do you want?' asked Bill Dick. 'In your dressing room,' he laughed.

'Funny,' I said, 'if a bit macabre. So when's the gig?'

'New Year's Eve,' he said. That particular date seemed to have a certain cloying familiarity about it, but so did numerous other things like music, motion pictures, and life on this planet.

Sometimes we do things that we don't understand. Like falling in love. Like riding a subway. Like eating a sandwich that's bigger than your head at the Carnegie Delicatessen.

After all, it was for God and country music. So I took a rather fatalistic puff on my cigar and I took the gig.

'A gig's a gig,' I said. I would play along with Bill Dick. I did not think the time was quite right to broach the subject of manila envelopes with big block letters.

It was closing in on two o'clock in the afternoon and it seemed to be warming up a bit. It was hard to tell what the weather was like when you never got off the telephone. I put on my cowboy hat and my hunting vest with the little rows of stitched pockets where some Americans keep their shotgun shells. I stuck a few cigars in the little pockets. What the hell? Best be prepared. I went outside.

Back in Texas it was hunting season. A good time to buy your mother-in-law a fur coat with antlers.

Now as I walked in the city, I could almost hear the random shots echoing off the Texas hills. What great sport to be a hunter. Kill things more beautiful than you. Shoot birds that flew higher than your dreams. Kill many buffalo. Once in a while you clean your gun and accidentally blow your head off. Good.

34

It was the night before Christmas. Visions of lonely, frozen bag ladies danced in my head. I'd burned out sugarplums the year before. Along with a few synapses.

I felt a little jumpy but fairly well rested. At least as well rested as I ever felt. I was still making up for the time I stayed awake for five years once in Nashville taking pills with colorful, almost lyrical names. That's what country music was all about. Ask ol' Hank.

I put a cassette on the stereo. Chinese children singing Christmas carols. Because of my years on the road, I did not normally like to hear the sound of human voices singing. But everyone, from time to time, requires a bit of auditory phenomenon. And you make do with what you got.

It was around tennish in the p.m., as they say in Hollywood, and I'd poured close to the last shot of whatever there used to be in the liquor cabinet. I lit a cigar and sat down in the rocker.

I was sitting there trying not to think about what I was obviously getting myself into when the phones rang. It was my sister Marcie calling from Berkeley, where she was studying fish. Not too many people study fish.

I'm sixteen years older than Marcie. Old enough to be her brother. When Marcie was about four I used to play tricks on her like older brothers will do. Told her Lassie'd died. Things like that.

Marcie was one of the few people younger than me whom I sometimes looked up to for wisdom and advice. Usually I never listened to younger people. I figured if they reached my age without hanging themselves from a shower rod, then I'd listen to them.

Marcie already knew a little bit about the 'troubles' at the Lone Star. She watched the *Today* show. The Hank Williams

Killer. The Lone Star Murders. I filled her in on the gory details as much as I could. Then I told her about the offer from Bill Dick.

She laughed. 'You didn't take it, did you?' she asked.

'Well,' I said. 'Well, see, I have an idea – '

'You didn't take it,' she said disbelievingly.

'Yes,' I said firmly. 'I took the gig.'

'That wasn't exactly best foot forward, Kinkster,' she said. I puffed patiently on my cigar.

'If I don't do it, it may mean the end of country music as we know it on this planet.' I knew she could relate to that. She was a George Jones fan. Hank Williams was like a brother to her.

Marcie didn't say anything. There was a long-distance silence on the line. If you've got to listen to silence, that's the best kind to have. I imagined a brightly colored tropical fish swimming by in an aquarium somewhere on the left coast and my sister watching it.

'Marcie,' I said, 'I know enough about this person to be pretty sure he's gonna make his move. And when he does, believe me, I'll be ready for him and well protected.' It didn't even sound too convincing to me.

'When's the show?' she asked.

'It's New Year's Eve,' I said.

'Do you know what day that is?' she asked in a voice turned suddenly cold.

'Yeah,' I said. 'I think it's a Wednesday.'

'That's not what I mean,' she said, a note of hysteria working its way in. 'New Year's Eve was the day Hank Williams died.'

I suppose subconsciously I'd known it all the time. I just hadn't thought about it, and I didn't want to think about it now. I picked up a Bic lighter that had been in the family

117

for about forty-eight hours and, fairly calmly, lit a fresh cigar.

'Yeah,' I said, 'there's that.'

It was about two o'clock in the morning when the phone rang for the last time. I was in the middle of an involved, vaguely sexual dream about my cat. I didn't know what the Freudian implications of it were, nor did I particularly care to find out. Like Frederick Exley said, 'What good are dreams if they come true?'

I didn't like the way the phone was ringing. As if it had a will of its own. It cut across the dark stillness of the room much louder than necessary. It sounded frantic and amoral. Like the voice of a medieval witch.

I hit the lights, picked up the receiver, and heard the mournful voice of Hank Williams. It sounded like a scratchy record and it probably was. Hank was singing from either hillbilly heaven or New York City, and at two o'clock in the morning either one was bad enough.

The song, I knew, was Hank's last hit while he was still alive. The words I heard were as follows:

> 'And brother, if I stepped on a worn-out dime
> I bet a nickel I could tell if it was heads or tails
> I'm not gonna worry wrinkles in my brow
> 'Cause nothin's ever gonna be alright nohow
> No matter how I struggle and strive
> I'll never get out of this world alive.'

I listened to see if there was any more. There wasn't. There didn't have to be.

I picked a half-smoked cigar out of the ashtray and stoked it up. I thought of Hank's primeval, mournful voice, and the more I thought about it, the more it seemed to be mourning for me. Just what I needed.

I got up a little shakily from the chair and walked over to the window. Outside the window I thought I heard a hoot owl call. In the distance, above the traffic, I was sure I could hear a lonesome whippoorwill.

Lonesome, however, was not my problem. My problem, it appeared, was that my three minutes were up. I poured another shot and carried it over to the window. I gazed with a sense of dread through the gloom at the rusty fire escapes across the street. I killed the shot.

It might've looked like I was smiling, but I wasn't. My lips were only sliding off my teeth.

All I'd got was a crank phone call. What the hell was there to worry about? Nobody'd sent me a song in a large manila envelope with big block letters yet.

But it's a funny thing when you're a songwriter. Sometimes you feel a song coming on.

35

It was Friday morning, the day after Christmas. Several hundred street-corner Santas were sleeping it off on the Bowery. The cat and I were in the loft, the espresso machine was gurgling, the garbage trucks were rumbling, and all was well in the world except that someone was making plans to kill me.

There'd been the 'I'll Never Get Out of This World Alive' phone call two nights before, and now there was a large manila envelope that had just come in the morning's mail and was sitting smugly square in the middle of my desk.

I didn't open it right away. Thought I'd leave myself something to do when the espresso was ready. Some guys read *The New York Times* as they sip their espresso in the morning. I open large manila envelopes with big block letters and read Hank Williams songs. Different strokes.

I took the envelope, poured a cup of espresso into my *Imus in the Morning* coffee mug, and sat down at the little table in the kitchen. The cat joined me by jumping up on top of the table. It was a good thing Ratso wasn't around. He didn't enjoy seeing cats on top of tables while people were sipping their espresso and reading their death threats. Thought it was a health hazard.

As I gingerly opened the envelope I could hear the lesbian dance class starting up directly over my head again. Strangely, I found it rather comforting. Like things were back to abnormal. I wished they were.

The song was 'Kaw-liga.' The wooden Indian.

If you were looking for a kink, pardon the expression, that might be attractive to a sick mind, you had a hell of a lot to work with in 'Kaw-liga.'

Some of the lyrics are as follows:

Kaw-liga was a wooden Indian standing by the door
He fell in love with an Indian maiden over in the
    antique store
Kaw-liga just stood there and never let it show
So she could never answer 'yes' or 'no.'

He always wore his Sunday feathers and held a
    tomahawk . . .

And then one day a wealthy customer bought the
    Indian maid
And took her, oh, so far away but ol' Kaw-liga stayed
Kaw-liga just stands there as lonely as can be
And wishes he was still an ol' pine tree

In fact, the story of 'Kaw-liga' is very appropriate to today's world. The futility, the miscommunications that govern life and love. If you can't empathize with Kaw-liga, you might as well not empathize at all.

I poured another cup of espresso and thought about poor ol' Kaw-liga. I knew a lot of guys like that. Knew a lot of Indian maidens. A lot of wealthy customers. I just didn't know which of my fine feathered friends was trying to kill me. I had about six days to find out who it was. It was scary, all right.

Somebody was trying to take my scalp before it got up and started crawling out the door.

In six days the Lord created the heavens and the earth and all the wonders therein. There are some of us who feel that He might have taken just a little more time.

Be that as it may, I had six days to marshal my troops, hammer out the plan, run some difficult background checks, establish what would have to pass for a rapport with Fox and Cooperman, research the data that I had – sparse and far afield as it was – and find the hidden architecture of the psyche, the twisted foundation stone of evil festering underneath the untold stories, the brick and mortar, the human facade.

Also, find the missing picture of Hank Williams, and keep Downtown Judy and Uptown Judy from bumping into each other on New Year's Eve.

Also, calibrate who was left-handed, and who, both as a child and as an adult, had been in the right place at the right time. Or the wrong place at the wrong time, depending how much of a moral judgment you wished to make.

Also, there were the usual household chores: buy cat food, toilet paper, cigars, and a bottle of Jameson. Not too many gourmet items. If I had any guests I could give them some of Bill Dick's Five-Alarm Chili, which by now looked like a hunk of black and silver frozen detritus but would probably appeal to most New Yorkers, who were constantly seeking something a little out of the ordinary.

Six days to get it all done. Christ, you could get hung up in traffic for six days. You could talk to an accountant at a cocktail party for six days. If you didn't know Leo, you could wait for a table at the Carnegie for six days.

Six days to enjoy life before you walk over a foggy little wooden bridge and meet a death's head coming at you from the other side. It was enough to make you wish you had a week.

I got the shopping done, fed the cat, and poured myself a bull's horn full of Jameson Irish Whiskey. I downed the shot.

I was trying to fit the toilet paper on the goddamn dispenser when the phones rang. It was 2.47 p.m. I could hear her accent even before I picked up the phone. It was Gunner.

She had been reading a lot of press about my New Year's Eve performance at the Lone Star and thought it 'very brave' of me to play the club. Would I be able to catch this Hank Williams person, she wanted to know.

I told her I was going to try unless at the last moment I woosied out and decided to take a French leave. She seemed to think it over for a few seconds. It was enough time for me to break out a new cigar and pop it into a rather vicious guillotine device given to me by my friends at the Smokehouse in Kerrville, Texas.

'Have you found my picture yet?' she asked. Interesting possessive pronoun, I thought. 'The Hank Williams person and the two boys?'

'Not yet,' I said.

'Humpf,' she said.

'Want to get together this week?' I asked.

'I'm very busy,' she said. 'Maybe after the show. You know, I've never seen you perform.'

'Musically speaking or any other way,' I said. 'Well, I may not make the show. It's kind of a country music tradition not to show up sometimes. Keeps the fans on their toes. George Jones does it a lot. So did the Hank Williams person.'

'If you don't play that show Wednesday night,' she said, enunciating very slowly and distinctly, 'you haven't got a hair on your bum.'

She hung up. Or rang off, as they say across the pond.

Maybe Gunner didn't appreciate the risk involved. Hell, maybe she did. Maybe the architecture of my personality was so displeasing to her she didn't give a bloody damn. At least two of the people she'd recently photographed at the Lone Star were now pushing up their various state flowers. I hadn't thought to ask her why she hadn't covered the Glaser Brothers show.

I puffed the cigar a bit and watched the cat, curled up, sleeping peacefully on a nearby chair. I decided I had to go through with it. I had to play the gig.

I'd never thought of myself as being particularly macho, but conversely, I didn't want anybody going around saying I didn't have a hair on my bum.

36

Rambam had had some success recently on a case in Washington, our nation's capital. He'd located a college kid from a prominent family who'd been missing and presumed spindled and mutilated by irritated Colombian drug-oriented individuals. Rambam found the kid alive and well, living out of his car and hiding from the Mob. Of course, now that he'd been found the kid could look forward to the life span of a mayfly, but nonetheless it was a feather in Rambam's cap.

I called Rambam and told him I needed a missing picture of Hank Williams found, hopefully in time to do me some good.

'Okay,' he said, 'where do I look?'

'I'm not sure yet,' I said, 'but I'll let you know.'

'Okay,' he said, 'when do I look?' Rambam, like most private eyes, always asked a lot of questions.

'New Year's Eve,' I said, 'while I'm onstage at the Lone Star.'

'I've got a date on New Year's Eve,' he said.

'Well,' I said, 'You'll have to make a moral choice between your gluttonous social life and the actual life or death of one of your close friends – me.'

'Let me think about it,' he said.

'There's the lad,' I said.

I hung up and called Ratso. Since he and Simmons seemed to be hitting it off so well, I'd asked him to do a little background work on the boy. We arranged to meet at the Derby at eight. I hung up and took a little power nap.

When I woke up I felt older and colder. I removed the cat litter box from the shower preparatory to getting in there myself. Power naps weren't what they used to be.

I got under the water and tried to shake off the gray, morphial threads. I started to feel pretty good. Not good enough to sing 'I'll Never Get Out of This World Alive,' but okay. I reflected upon what Conrad Hilton, the great hotel magnate, had said when someone asked him what he'd learned in his many years on the planet. He'd said: 'Always keep the shower curtain inside the tub.'

I followed his advice.

Before I left for the Derby I made a condolence call to Tompall Glaser at his top-secret, unpublished number in Nashville. His phone number was about the only thing unpublished about Tompall. He and his surviving brothers, Chuck and Jim, owned one of the biggest publishing houses in Nashville. They'd published many of my early songs as well. We were still on speaking terms.

'Sorry, hoss,' I said when Tompall picked up the phone, 'about Ned.'

'Yeah,' he said in a voice that John Wayne would have been proud of, 'Chuck and Jim are kind of sorry, too. They're sorry it wasn't me.' He laughed a raw laugh, more hollow than hearty. 'I'll miss the little bastard.'

In spite of the Glaser Brothers' legendary feuding, I rather thought he would. I didn't say anything.

'Why,' asked Tompall, 'do you think he picked on Ned?'

'I'm going to find out,' I said. 'I'm playing the Lone Star on New Year's Eve.'

'Jesus,' Tompall said. 'You've got pawnshop balls, brother.' There was a pause.

'Hey,' he said, 'Captain Midnite's here. Wants to talk to you. Thanks for calling, Kinky.' I heard Tompall filling Midnite in on my forthcoming performance at the Lone Star.

'If anything happens to you,' said Midnite as he came on the line, 'can I have your saddle?'

'Cowboys today don't have saddles,' I said. 'We have answering machines, VCRs, word processors.'

'How about your catalogue?' he asked.

'Midnite,' I said, 'you realize I may really fucking die next week.'

'Yeah,' he said, 'I thought about that. In fact, I think about you a lot.' I hadn't seen Midnite in seven years, but I still felt close to him. That was probably the secret of maintaining a friendship in country music. Stay the hell away from each other.

'Just watch your ass,' he said in a softer tone. 'I'm playing golf next week, and if anything happens to you – you know what they say.'

'No, I don't know what they say,' I said.

'You can't putt with a broken heart,' said Captain Midnite.

37

Ratso and I had just dusted off two big hairys at the Derby and were now drinking coffee escorted by sambuca, which Andrew himself brought to us in appropriately stemmed glasses. I admired Andrew for never commenting on Ratso's sartorial situation. Ratso was wearing dead man's shoes, fuchsia pants, and a coonskin cap with the tail and with the little face of the raccoon mounted on the front of it. The eyes were sewn shut, and the damn thing looked pretty hideous even if you weren't a liberal.

'How's it going, Kinky?' Andrew asked in his gracious tones.

'It's going all right, Andrew,' I said.

'Good,' said Andrew. 'The sambuca's on the house.'

'Now it's going better,' I said. I picked a coffee bean out of the glass and chewed on it. If you've never eaten a coffee bean out of a glass of sambuca you've never lived.

'Ratso,' I said, 'before we go over the minutes of our last Rotarian meeting, I'd like to ask you to please remove your hat. Not that it isn't attractive, but that dead little face keeps reminding me of what I might look like Thursday morning if anything goes wrong with my plan.'

'No problem,' said Ratso, and he put the hat on the rack behind him in such a manner that the sewn eye slits appeared to glare evilly at the woman at the next table. The woman glared back at the little hat with an expression as void of life and as unpleasant as the dead raccoon. Then she looked at Ratso.

'Disgusting,' she said.

Ratso looked briefly at the woman, the hat, and then the woman again.

'Don't feed it,' he said. I took another coffee bean out of my sambuca and chewed it thoughtfully.

'Here's the deal, Ratso,' I said. 'We're amateurs, but we're smart. We have basic psychological profiles of a number of acquaintances of ours. We've got this knowledge firsthand, from knowing these people for some time. But does anybody really ever get to know anybody?

'We've got clues, details, background information. More than we need. We've got to go at it from a different angle than the cops. The guy we're looking for is very smart. Got a Ph.D. in evil. You understand?'

Ratso nodded solemnly. His gaze wandered over to a dessert tray in the corner.

'On Wednesday night,' I continued, 'I've got to drop the mask from one of these guys before one of these guys drops a death mask on me. I'll need you, Rambam, Boris, and anybody else you can think of.'

'The Village Irregulars,' Ratso said. 'Will that be enough?' I shrugged.

'I'm talking to Fox and Cooperman tomorrow,' I said.

'We'll be ready,' Ratso said. 'We just don't know what we're gonna be ready for.'

'I've got a fairly good idea, I'm afraid,' I said. I took the sheet music to 'Kaw-liga' and the Big Chief tablet out of my coat pocket. I filled Ratso in on everything I knew. It didn't take long.

When I finished, Ratso made some notes to himself on a few pieces of Chelsea Hotel stationery. 'You don't miss much,' I said.

'I just wanted to get down a few details,' said Ratso.

'No,' I said, 'I mean lifting the Chelsea Hotel stationery.'

'C'mon,' said Ratso, 'it's very high camp.'

'What did you find out about Simmons?' I asked.

'Interesting,' he said. 'I got this from Simmons' brother,

Andy. He's a couple years younger than Mike. The two of them have always been very close. Simmons is quite frustrated apparently. Hasn't gotten where he wants in country music.'

'Who has?' I asked. Everybody wanted to be Hank Williams but nobody wanted to die.

'Anyway,' Ratso said, 'this Texas background of his is pretty bogus. He lived there all of six months once. Been a Yankee almost all of his life and won't even admit it to himself.'

'Yeah,' I said.

'He's had it rough,' said Ratso. 'Not many breaks. Never played the Opry. About ten years ago he performed for a while on the Wheeling Jamboree in Wheeling, West Virginia.' He paused to slurp his coffee. 'That's hard work.'

'What is?' I asked.

'Wheeling, West Virginia,' said Ratso. He laughed.

'That's pretty goddamn funny,' I said. I thought about it for a moment. I knocked off the sambuca distractedly and said, 'Very curious, my dear Ratso.'

'What do you mean?' he asked.

'West Virginia,' I said. 'It keeps popping up. Simmons has lived there. Cleve. Flippo.' I signaled the waiter for more coffee and a couple more sambucas. Ratso ordered a walnut-apple-pecan cake, the house's specialty.

'I'm reading a very strange book,' said Ratso, 'by John Keel, a top authority on UFOs and a personal friend of mine. The book's called *The Mothman Prophecies* and it's about these ten-foot-tall winged creatures that thousands of people have reportedly seen in the skies over West Virginia.'

'At least it's not about Hitler, Bob Dylan, or Jesus,' I said.

Ratso attacked the walnut-apple-pecan cake, unfazed by my remark. When he'd knocked off a good bit, and with his mouth still not quite empty, he said, 'West Virginia is one of the very few places in the country that the Indians never fought over. Keel suggests it was a cursed land, a haunted area, maybe a burial ground of some kind.'

'Nice place to get a postcard from, right?' I asked.

'Right,' said Ratso. 'It's sort of a bad-karma place.'

'It sure was for Hank,' I said.

'Why was that?' Ratso asked.

'Hank died there,' I said.

38

McGovern had said it was very important that we meet for a breakfast engagement at ten o'clock Saturday morning at the LaLobotomy Coffee Shop on Eighth Avenue. The place's actual name was LaBonbonniere, but a gorgeous girlfriend of mine, The Lizard, had named it LaLobotomy and the name had stuck. It fit the clientele pretty well, including the way I felt myself that morning.

In spite of the fact that it was already ten-thirty and that McGovern's house was only one block away on Jane Street, McGovern was not there. Big surprise.

Charles, the owner, brought me a cup of coffee and a large glass of tomato juice without my having to order it. Charles was a real rarity, an extremely likable Frenchman, but the food was pure American greasy spoon. Best breakfast place in New York. Excluding dim sum, of course.

I was drinking my coffee and reading the *New York Post* when I suddenly saw McGovern looming in the doorway of the little place. He looked about four times as big as God.

'Hey, great,' he said. 'I thought I missed you.'

'I'm afraid not,' I said. 'Have a rough night?'

'Who?' asked McGovern. 'Me?' His hearty Irish laughter filled the little place to the point where a startled young homosexual couple and an incipient bag lady looked over at our table. McGovern was already perusing the menu and didn't notice. I returned their gaze with calm dignity. Saint Kinky. Patron saint and defender of large, exuberant Irishmen in small Village coffee shops.

Charles brought coffee for McGovern and took both our orders. McGovern and I drank our coffee and watched the world go by outside the windows of LaLobotomy. He'd brought a copy of the *Daily News* with him, and I of course had the *Post*. If conversation lagged, there was always reality. Or we could read the newspapers.

I didn't feel too bad bringing the *Post* with me knowing, of course, that McGovern wrote for the *Daily News*. It made him feel superior and just a little smug to be having breakfast with a *Post* reader. I liked to be supportive of my friends.

'Your show at the Lone Star,' said McGovern. 'They want me to do a feature on it. I know it's hard for you to give up all this press, but I think you ought to get out of it while you still can. I've got a bad feeling about it. I say cancel the show.' McGovern looked un-McGovernly serious.

I sipped my coffee and watched a blind man, two identically dressed homosexuals, and a nun cross Eighth Avenue against the light. Could've made a citizen's arrest but I thought I'd let it slide.

'What the hell's so funny?' asked McGovern.

'I keep looking at these damn people outside the window,' I said. 'They look like discarded lines from old Bob Dylan songs.'

'You're sure that's not your reflection you're seeing?' asked McGovern. He laughed again. A little too loud, I thought, for the small restaurant.

'Could well be, McGovern,' I said. 'I'm an aristocratic freak. I've earned my right to be here.'

'Good,' said McGovern. 'So you'll cancel the gig?'

'Of course not,' I said. 'It's very important that I play this gig. In the words of Thomas Paine, "I care not who makes a country's laws, if I can write her songs." ' I finished my coffee and looked at McGovern.

He got his coat off the floor and stood up to go. 'You may write the songs,' he said, shaking his big, handsome head sadly, 'but I write the obituaries.'

39

I walked the ten bone-chilling blocks to the cop shop. The world outside was not as warm and cozy as Charles' little coffee shop. I just hoped heaven looked like LaLobotomy. I looked at the street. The garbage cans whose lids runneth over. The stray dogs. Stray people. Everything was as cold as a bank lobby on the South Pole. Almost made you wish you lived in West Virginia.

The green globes of the Sixth Precinct suddenly came upon me. I felt a twinge of something akin to guilt. Maybe like a hot dog vendor operating without a licence. Cooperman and Fox and I did not have an especially sharing and caring relationship. The only evidence I was legally withholding was the song 'Lost Highway' that Rambam had lifted from Bill Dick's desk. I had 'Lost Highway' in my coat pocket, but it'd be hard to explain without implicating Rambam, and I needed Rambam. I had such a complicated code of ethics that quite often I couldn't even crack it myself.

I gave my name to the guy who was nodding out at the muster desk, and I took a seat in a little plastic chair with a small writing arm on it. The chair was screwed into the floor tighter than the Statue of Liberty. There was another guy sitting in a similar chair in the corner. He had a mental-hospital haircut and his eyes seemed to be rolling back into his head a little more than was fashionable. One of his hands was handcuffed to the arm of the chair. Looked like he was waiting, too.

They called my number first.

I walked into the valley of death to face Cooperman and his coffee cup. Fox wasn't there. I didn't ask after him.

'Sit down,' said Cooperman. I sat down.

'What do you take in your coffee, Senator?' he asked.

'Everything,' I said.

He took his own cup, found another one on a nearby desk, and walked over to a Mr Coffee machine in the corner. 'I'll bet,' he said.

I thought of the night, several months ago, before all this had started, when Ratso and I had been driving down Seventh Avenue and had seen Joe DiMaggio walking into the Carnegie Delicatessen at one-thirty in the morning.

'Jesus,' said Ratso, 'there he is.'

'Yeah,' I said, 'looks like he's alone.'

'Well,' said Ratso, 'he's not with Marilyn.'

Joe walked into the Carnegie, and Ratso and I turned the corner at the light. 'Nobody is,' I said.

'You know,' said Ratso, 'I hear kids still swarm him for autographs, but they say, "Mr Coffee! Mr Coffee!" They don't even know he's Joe fucking DiMaggio.' We drove through several blocks of teeming loneliness ... Kentucky Fried Chicken ... a hooker or two ... an empty skyscraper.

'I hope to Christ he gets linen,' I said.

Cooperman placed the coffee in front of me and sat down heavily in a beat-up office chair on the other side of the desk.

'What's on your mind?' he asked.

Cooperman was not especially pleased to learn of my upcoming New Year's Eve gig at the Lone Star Cafe. He was even less happy to learn that the song 'Lost Highway,' which

I'd placed on the desk between us, had been given to me by Frank Serpico.

'Christ, that's a good one,' said Cooperman with a very unpleasant little fixed-wing smile on his face.

'Yeah,' I said. 'It was found in Bill Dick's desk – no postmark, the envelope unopened – the night Ned Glaser died.'

'Do tell,' said Cooperman sweetly. 'It's so nice to have this information.' He took a sip of coffee. He smiled a big smile. It was the kind of smile that in a million years might have reached his eyes. I didn't have the time to wait.

'I got a song as well, in the mail this week,' I said. 'Ever hear of "Kaw-liga"?'

'Black Muslim leader?' Cooperman asked.

I took a sip of my coffee and winced slightly. 'No,' I said. 'Kaw-liga was a wooden Indian standing by the door. He fell in love with an Indian maiden over in the antique store.'

'And?' said Cooperman.

'And – you know,' I said. 'Boy meets girl, boy loses girl, country singer loses life. Same old story.' We both sipped our coffee.

'Okay,' said Cooperman, 'Let's have it. What have you got? Any more withheld evidence? Any hare-brained theories? Any ideas at all? Let's hear 'em.' Cooperman leaned back in his chair. He took a Gauloise out of the pack on the desk and lighted it with a Zippo. I took a cigar out of my hunting vest and, in my coat pocket, found a pink Bic lighter. This one had only been in the family about twelve hours. I began the prenuptial arrangements on the cigar and I told Cooperman what I knew.

'Look,' he said in a tired voice, 'we now have three victims, all of them in some way involved with the Lone Star Cafe. They work there, they play there, the point is, they die there. With the exception of Glaser, who died on the West Side Highway. Now we got this baby stashed in

Bill Dick's desk.' He gestured with his hand to the song 'Lost Highway,' and an ash from his Gauloise fell on Hank's lyrics like a big gray teardrop. Nobody brushed it away. Even the French probably would've liked Hank Williams, I thought. If they ever stopped thinking about Jerry Lewis long enough.

'Then we got you,' continued Cooperman, 'playing this show New Year's Eve at the goddamn Lone Star Cafe like a decoy cop calling in his backup unit. That what you're doin'?'

'Well,' I said.

'Well, let me tell you, friend. The backup may not be enough.'

I puffed on my cigar and started to say something, but Cooperman went on. 'Then we got a perpetrator running around reading all the papers and watching the eleven o'clock news, gettin' his balls all pumped up.'

Cooperman studied me for a bit longer than was pleasant, then he asked. 'Ever been to a Christmas party in a ward for the criminally insane?'

'Not yet,' I said.

Cooperman lit another frog butt and squinted at me through the smoke. 'You're out on a limb, my man,' he said. 'You got yourself into this one. We'll be there Wednesday night, but I don't envy you, Tex.' He smiled.

With a modified papal sign he signified that the interview was over. I headed for the door. I had the feeling that the lines were down. Very little I'd told him had gotten through. And if he knew much about the case, he wasn't saying. So much for sharing and caring.

By the time I left, the guy that had been handcuffed to the plastic chair was gone. I wondered who the hell he thought *he* was. Maybe he knew who he was and that's why he'd had to be handcuffed to a plastic chair. Maybe the only way to save ourselves was to handcuff the whole world to a plastic chair. But there weren't enough handcuffs and there weren't enough plastic chairs. And there'd be nobody left to throw away the key. Otherwise, the idea was pretty sound.

It was raining lightly as I made my way over to 199B Vandam. Christmas had come and gone like an elf out of hell. I was beginning to feel progressively more like worm bait the closer I got to Wednesday night. I hoped it wasn't going to spoil my weekend.

As I walked through the cold I thought of something F. Scott Fitzgerald had said in *Tender Is the Night*. It was to the effect that everybody in France thinks he's Napoleon and everybody in Italy thinks he's Christ.

Well, you could chalk up another one for the Big Apple. Somebody in New York evidently thought he was Hank Williams.

40

For a horrifying, lucid moment I didn't know who I was or where I was. It was a bit like knowing what goes on in the mind of a game show host. Not a pleasant experience.

It was Saturday night. Sitting Bull was looking at me from the cover of the Big Chief tablet, which was lying on the floor. I picked him up. I sat him on the table.

The Big Chief tablet didn't have a hell of a lot to tell me. Just a very abbreviated biography of some of the people I'd been checking up on and a hurried transcript of mostly incoherent comments they'd made. My handwriting looked like the handwriting of a mouse.

'Which one of you isn't what you seem to be?' I said to the cat. The cat didn't say anything.

'Which one of you is really a fiend disguised as a friend?'

Was that even possible? Well, friends, it sure looked that way. Of course, looks can be deceiving. But then again, so could friends.

From Simmons I had: '. . . grew up in Texas. Where do you think I got my Texas accent?' Simmons didn't have a Texas accent, but he thought he did. People in New York thought he had one, too, but what did they know? The way he sang was Texas, but the way he spoke wouldn't have racked up too many points with the boys in the bunkhouse.

Simmons continued: 'When we were kids Dad used to take us down to the Grand Ol' Opry, and I guess some of it must've rubbed off.'

Bill Dick had denied any knowledge of the manila envelope that Rambam found in his desk. I didn't want to push it just yet. Maybe he'd only hidden the envelope in his desk and not shown it to the Glaser Brothers so they wouldn't cancel their gig. A coward, not a killer. But there were other possibilities that presented themselves. When I asked him where he'd grown up he said, 'Born and raised in Brooklyn, New York.' Asked if he'd ever been in the South, he said with some little pride, 'Never been below the Mason-Dixon line.' Of course, I thought, Billy the Kid had been born and raised in Brooklyn, too.

Cleve was very unhappy at the Lone Star. Understandably so, I thought. We talked and laughed about some of the years on the road when he'd been road manager for my band. Those times were miserable enough, but now they seemed like the good ol' days. We reminisced about a country western Bar Mitzvah we'd played together in New Jersey some years back. It had been a cocaine nightmare – backyard swimming pool, bales of hay, kids with cap guns in little cowboy suits running around everywhere.

I thought of the two little kids Gunner had told me about

in the photograph I'd never seen. More than ever I felt it was important.

I'd gotten Cleve's background down for the hell of it. 'We grew up in Kentucky . . . moved to Virginia, West Virginia, Tennessee, Texas – you name it.' Cleve was an only child, he said. He'd been on the circuit for a while. He thought working at the Lone Star would bring him some peace of mind. Surprise.

It wasn't written down on the Big Chief tablet, but Cleve had expressed grave concern about my playing the Lone Star on New Year's Eve. He'd said it was a crazy idea of Bill Dick's and he'd advised me to think seriously about pulling out of the gig.

'A gig's a gig,' I'd told him.

'You're a fucking idiot,' he'd said.

Chet Flippo grew up in Ohio. Lived in Texas, Tennesse, West Virginia, Texas again, and finally married and moved to New York. Had a brother a couple of years older and a little sister. Thought he was going to give himself a nervous breakdown while writing *Your Cheatin' Heart: A Biography of Hank Williams*. Seems the boy overidentified with his field of study – thought he was Hank and his wife was Audrey.

Flippo had one rather interesting thing to say. On New Year's Day 1953, when he was ten years old, he remembered waiting for a long time in a big hall in Canton, Ohio, to see a show by Hank Williams. That was the show Hank never played. Somebody'd made an announcement that Hank had died. The band played 'I Saw the Light' from behind a closed curtain at the back of the stage. People who were there, Flippo said, never forgot it. That great emptiness. That sense of loss. Flippo had been fascinated with Hank ever since.

You want to be a country music hero, you've got to die at precisely the right time. And Hank's timing was damn

137

near perfect. For everybody but him. He was only twenty-nine years old. But then again, old age wasn't usually very pleasant and it didn't necessarily ensure any measure of greatness. I thought of what Will Rogers, another guy with a sense of timing, had once said: 'Longevity has ruined as many men as it's made.' Of course, the way I was living, it didn't look like that was going to be my problem.

So that was the Big Chief tablet. A little geography, a little ancient history, a little psychology. Of course, I wasn't a psychologist. But I could tell a person whose Otis box wasn't rising to the penthouse. And I could put pieces together. A few pieces were starting to fit into the picture. But the picture, unfortunately, was still missing.

I thought of Gunner. I'd tried to call her the night before but her machine was on. Listening to it made you want to have sexual relations with her accent.

Couldn't be too careful in the psycho serial-murder business. Even when dealing with women, foreigners, or friends. Satan was an equal opportunity employer.

I tried to think of other suspects, someone I'd overlooked, but it just didn't fit. I was sure that one of them had to be involved. A perfect stranger couldn't have wreaked this much havoc. Too inside. Too meticulous. Too . . . intelligent.

I had a little trouble getting back to sleep. It seemed that Intimations of Mortality and Morpheus were armwrestling with each other on the bridge of my nose. Both would get their chance, I figured, so I didn't worry about it too much.

Just before I got back to sleep, only two thoughts were going through my head. Who would feed the cat if something happened to me? was the first one. The second one was, if a lesbian dance class was thudding on the ceiling and there was nobody in the loft below to hear it, would it make any noise?

41

It's almost as hard to get good Mexican food in New York as it is in Mexico. You've got to know what you're doing in this world or life passes you by. My pal Joel Siegel and I thought about it a while and finally opted for barbecue.

Joel took me to Smokey's on Twenty-fourth Street and Ninth Avenue. It wasn't bad for New York. But it wasn't Howie's #1.

Afterward, I stopped by Ratso's apartment. Somewhere in Ratso's apartment you could find everything in the world – a nonfunctional exercise bike, a four-foot-tall statue of the Virgin Mary, a stuffed polar bear's head, and over two hundred slightly used hockey sticks.

I browsed through Ratso's vast library of books – mostly about Jesus, Bob Dylan, and Hitler – until I found what I was looking for. An old AAA road map of the United States. Circa 1953.

It was still early when I got back to 199B Vandam but it was already almost dark. It was that lonely time in New York or anyplace else just before Sunday night becomes Sunday night. I was looking at Ratso's road atlas and smoking a two dollar and seventy-five-cent Upmann cigar. The same kind John Kennedy smoked. I wondered what kind Adlai Stevenson would've smoked if he'd been elected President. Ah, well . . .

It was 7.52 in New York; 4.52 in California. Three hours difference in time and a few cultural differences I won't go into. As a general rule of thumb, however, if you thought of New York as a Negro talking to himself and of California as a VCR with nothing to put in it, you wouldn't be too far off the mark.

'Charlie,' I said, 'I got a little problem.' Charles Ansell was an old friend of the family. He was also the head shrink of the San Fernando Valley and one of the foremost world authorities on sibling rivalry, dream analysis, and Lenny Bruce. He was also, so my father claims, the first man he'd ever seen hold a cigarette lighter up to his ass and light a fart.

'You just think you've got a problem,' Charlie said. 'After all the shit I've listened to today, you couldn't have a problem.' I familiarized him with the situation.

'You've got a problem,' he said.

As Charlie talked I jotted down anything I felt was remotely pertinent into my Big Chief tablet. He laid it out clearly so a fairly hip layman like myself could understand. Not too many twenty-dollar words.

'Does that help?' he asked when he finished.

'I'll let you know Thursday morning,' I said. I started to hang up and then I thought of something. 'Oh, Charlie,' I said, 'sometime ago I had a dream –'

'You think you're Martin Luther King,' he said.

'This is relatively serious, Charlie,' I said, 'and the price is right, so let me ask your opinion about it.' I told Charlie about the dream in which I'd found the miniature baby with the diaper the size of a commemorative stamp. I told him how all my friends gathered around and began insisting that the diaper be changed and how no one had seen fit to comment on the ridiculously small size of the infant.

'It means that I think I have a small penis, right?' I asked. I knew this wasn't remotely true, but it seemed to me to be a classic interpretation.

'No,' said Charlie, 'it doesn't mean that at all.' I blew a relieved cloud of smoke up toward the ceiling in the general direction of the lesbian dance class.

'Well, then what the hell *does* it mean?' I asked.

'It means your friends are stupid,' he said.

42

It was that hour when the prince's coach turns into a gypsy cab smelling strongly of ganja. I wandered across Seventh Avenue and stepped down into the Monkey's Paw with my Big Chief tablet and Ratso's ancient AAA road atlas firmly under my arm and a lit cigar firmly under my upper lip. A frowsy woman at the bar made frantic little fanning gestures with her hand in the direction of my cigar. I ignored her.

Ratso had said he would meet me but I didn't see him yet. Maybe he was inventorying his apartment. Mick Brennan was there and appeared to be a few drinks ahead of me.

'Where's Michael Caine?' I asked as I ordered a Bushmills Irish Whiskey instead of Jameson Irish Whiskey. Thought I'd try a little variation on a theme.

'Michael,' said Brennan laughing, 'is over talking to your friend Cleve at the Lone Star, trying to get a booking. He's envious of all the press you're getting.'

I downed the shot of Bushmills. It wasn't noticeably different from Jameson. Of course, who could tell with one shot? 'That's fairly cosmic,' I said. 'Michael Caine is the one guy I'm envious of. I mean, if I couldn't be me, I'd like to be him.'

'Tell him when I see him,' said Brennan.

'Mick,' I said, 'I've got another photographic query for you. This one goes back some years.' I posed the problem to Mick and he confirmed what I'd already suspected. It didn't tell me much about the identity of the killer, but it was another piece in the puzzle of the missing Hank Williams picture.

Mick drifted away. I had another shot of Bushmills. I watched The Weasel, the local purveyor of marching powder, scurry back and forth from the men's room. I strayed at the bar and waited for Ratso. Satan, get thee away from my left nostril.

I was drinking a Bass ale and looking at the Alabama-Tennessee-Virginia-West Virginia section of the road atlas when I felt a presence at my left shoulder. Ratso and Boris. Boris was a Russian karate expert who could kill you in over a hundred ways without leaving any marks. Ratso reached over, took the glass out of my hand, and drank off a good portion of the Bass ale.

'Not bad,' he said.

'It's only a cold sore,' I said. 'Don't worry, I'll check it out at the free clinic next week.'

Boris, who rarely drank liquor, said, 'To-ma-to juice' to the bartender in a dangerous-sounding, almost lethal accent. He smiled the kind of smile you smile when you know you can kill a man in over a hundred ways without leaving any marks.

I looked back at the road atlas and said, 'Montgomery, Chattanooga, Knoxville, Rutledge, Bristol, Cedarville, Chilhowie, Marion, Wytheville, Bluefield, Princeton, Beckley, Willis Branch, Oak Hill.'

'Zame to you,' said Boris.

'Actually,' I said, 'eighty-six Montgomery and Chattanooga. We're only talkin' Knoxville, Rutledge, Bristol, Cedarville, Chilhowie, Marion, Wytheville, Bluefield, Princeton, Beckley, Willis Branch, and Oak Hill.'

'That's better,' said Boris grimly.

'Boris,' I said, 'I don't expect a person of your rich Eastern background to understand – '

'Murder?' Boris laughed. 'I have seen much, much murder.' His eyes were not laughing. They were gray and silent as the snow falling over Leningrad.

'So what's with all the little hick towns?' Ratso asked.

'They're not little hick towns, Ratso,' I said. 'They're just not New York.' I drank what was left of my Bass ale.

'That's what I said,' said Ratso.

'I'm working,' I said, 'on Hank Williams's last ride.' I signaled Tommy for another Bushmills and another Bass ale. 'Now, according to the date on that missing photograph, as Gunner remembers it – she should, it's her mum's birthday – we can probably exclude Knoxville, too.'

Ratso bent over the bar to study the road atlas. He loved maps. I hated maps. Unless they had pins in them and were on the Pentagon wall and I was indicating with a pointer to our government leaders where I believed the giant ants would first attack the earth. I hated maps. Boris maintained a polite interest and drank his tomato juice.

'That leaves eleven little hick towns, as you say, Ratso, that Hank passed through on the last night of his life: Rutledge, Bristol, Cedarville, Chilhowie, Marion, Wytheville, Bluefield – '

'All right, all right,' said Ratso irritably. 'Give it a rest. What's the point of the exercise?'

'The point, Ratso,' I said a bit unkindly, 'is right on top of your head.' I downed the shot.

'C'mon, c'mon,' said Ratso impatiently. 'What's the point of knowing all these little towns that Hank passed through?'

'There was a photograph of Hank taken by someone in one of these towns. That's the photograph that's now missing from the Lone Star Cafe, and I believe it's central to the case. It's a photo of two small boys and Hank at Howie's #1 BBQ, dated December 31, 1952. It's a slim lead, but if we can find the town we can check the courthouse records, if they have them, and verify which of our little friends was there at the time.'

'Long shot,' said Ratso. Unfortunately, he was right. And time was running out.

Boris had another tomato juice, decided he'd stop at two, and left, promising to be at the Lone Star on Wednesday night.

'There is one more thing, Ratso,' I said as we sat at the bar, the AAA road atlas lying forlornly in front of us like a forgotten woman. I opened the Big Chief tablet to the notes I'd made of my call to Charles Ansell. 'The head shrink of the San Fernando Valley says it's hard to "decode the fantasy of a psychopath." Says often they'll "merge – become another person." He says "time doesn't phase a psychopath, they're timeless, they never get over it. There's an initial trauma that they've never recovered from. Such as, a guy sees his mother hang herself and years later he hangs his wife." '

'That's understandable,' said Ratso. We got another round from Tommy.

'Okay,' I said, 'Ansell says there seems to be a "self-imposed guilt situation." What brings it about we don't know. But in the killer's case, the trauma almost certainly had its origins in childhood and has, in Ansell's words, "kept him as a kid." '

'Sounds like you,' said Ratso.

'Also,' I said, 'he's fixated with a need not to let anyone eclipse Hank's success. He's Hank reincarnate. He feels threatened as he feels Hank would've felt threatened. Basic motivations for murder, we understand. Greed, jealousy, et cetera. But psychological motivations are much more difficult to comprehend. That's what Ansell says. I say it adds up to an ugly surprise and a rather tedious wig.'

'You should've been a psychologist,' said Ratso. 'You missed your calling.'

'Maybe I was out playing miniature golf,' I said.

I was getting cigar ashes on the road atlas. It was damn

near three o'clock in the morning. On my most recent trip to the men's room I happened to glimpse my face in the mirror. My eyes were starting to look like road atlases, too. Old ones with a lot of roads and highways that weren't even there anymore.

I was still drinking but I wasn't thinking. Ratso was talking to the woman who hadn't liked my cigar smoke. Mick Brennan drifted over, put a cold mug of Heineken down right in the middle of my AAA road atlas, and headed for the men's room.

'Goddammit, Brennan,' I said. I removed the mug from the surface of the map. There was a dark circle where it had been. It extended all the way from Chilhowie to Oak Hill. I stared dumbly at the circle for a moment. Then I said: 'Jesus Christ . . . Ratso . . . that's it. I've got it.' I smiled a slightly crooked smile into the mirror behind the bar.

'What do you have?' Ratso asked. 'Besides herpes, I mean.'

I folded up the road atlas and gathered up the Big Chief tablet. 'I've got the answer,' I said. 'I'll verify it first thing in the morning, and then Wednesday night I'll try to snare this unsavory little booger.' I stood up a little shakily and put twenty bucks on the bar. I was wired and inspired.

'I'm glad,' said Ratso a little unconvincingly, 'but Sherlock, do you have to get so fucked up to solve a case?'

The woman who hadn't liked my cigar smoke had vanished into thin air in the fashion of cigar smoke. Other, much dearer people had disappeared from my life in almost the same way.

'My dear Ratso,' I said, 'you know what Oscar Wilde had to say, don't you?'

'No,' said Ratso, 'what'd he say?'

' "All of us are lying in the gutter, but some of us are looking at the stars." '

43

I made a brief flurry of phone calls early Monday morning. I called the office of the county clerk in the court-house of a little country seat in Virginia. Yes, Virginia, there is a person in New York who thinks he's Hank Williams and is going around killing people. Yes, Virginia, there've been three stiffs already connected with the Lone Star Cafe, and now I'm going to perform there myself. Yes, Virginia, smart move.

I got the information I wanted from Virginia, and I was a little surprised about what I'd learned. Just a *little* surprised.

I called my brother, Roger, who lived in Maryland, and invited him to the show on New Year's Eve. It was arranged that he'd come right to the Lone Star from Penn Station and meet me there. I called Cleve to alert him that Roger was coming and to put him on my hit list at the door. I called Rambam and told him when and where he should look for the missing picture.

Then I thought about what I was getting myself into, and I damn near panicked.

A jolt of Jameson settled me down a bit. If I left New York now I would still have to come back and show my face sometime, and that would be difficult. Once you've lived in New York City you can't really get away. It keeps calling you back, like a perverse Hawaii.

I would stay, I decided. Didn't want anybody calling me a woosy. Didn't want anybody saying I didn't have a hair on my bum. Of course, if anything went wrong, those would be two fairly stupid reasons to die. I'd have to chance it.

But in the event that I was killed or incapacitated, who would take care of the cat?

I called Ratso. He didn't want the cat. Even for just a few days. He was worried about the cat pissing on his ten thousand books relating to Jesus, Bob Dylan, and Hitler. I told him that sooner or later, cats piss on everything. Later, he said. Some friend.

I started to call McGovern but thought better of it. You couldn't in good conscience leave a cat with McGovern. You wouldn't want to do that to a dog.

I called Mick Brennan.

'Mick,' I said, 'would you mind keeping the cat for a few days?'

'Not on your life, mate,' he said in a quiet, serious voice.

'Thanks a lot,' I said, 'you self-directed, me-generation bastard.' All my friends were really coming through for me.

'Look, mate,' said Brennan, 'who's the lesbian bird that runs the dance class in the loft above yours?'

'Winnie Katz,' I said irritably. 'What's it to you?'

'Nothing to me, mate,' he said, 'but she might not mind having a little pussy around.' Brennan laughed. I thought about it. It had a lot of advantages. It certainly beat putting the cat in a pillowcase and lugging her eighty blocks uptown, fighting and scratching all the way in the back of a cab like I used to do.

I thanked Mick and hung up, and I called Winnie. She answered the phone slightly out of breath. None of my business.

'Winnie?'

'Yes?'

'This is Kinky downstairs.'

'Yes?' I hoped I wasn't interrupting the class or anything.

'I may be out of pocket for a few days. I wondered if you'd mind keeping my cat while I'm gone?'

There was a silence on the phone for a moment. Then she asked, 'Is the cat a female?'

'Of course,' I said.

'I wouldn't want a tomcat up here spraying the whole place. Scratching up the balance beams.'

'I know what you mean,' I said disapprovingly.

There was another silence. This time a little longer. Then she said, 'Okay, I'll take her.' Interesting choice of words.

'Great,' I said. 'This is Monday. I'll drop her off with you Wednesday morning.' I thanked her again and hung up.

The cat was sleeping on the desk under her heat lamp. I patted her on the head and said, 'You're gonna have a great time. You'll be in good, safe, experienced hands. Now you won't have to ride inside a pillowcase in the back of a taxi with your eyes turning green and flashing like Satan. It's all for the best. Trust me.'

The cat went back to sleep. I lit a cigar and dialed Uptown Judy. We agreed to get together that evening at the loft. I hung up.

44

Uptown Judy's recording of *Carmen* was on my stereo. Uptown Judy was on my bed. She was wearing a blue robe that fell open occasionally to reveal powder-blue panties. I liked girls with a good sense of color coordination.

I was wearing a West Point sweatshirt and my old sarong from Borneo. A heady combination of toughness and sensitivity, so important in today's world.

I turned off the light, walked over to the bed, took off the sweatshirt and sarong. In the dimness I could see the cat sleeping, almost poignantly, on top of my suitcase. I got under the covers. Uptown Judy had disrobed, so to speak, and now she struggled out of the panties and pitched them into the darkness.

I slid over a little closer to her.

'Closer,' she said.

'I can't get any closer without performing the Heimlich maneuver,' I said.

If you are firmly enough rooted in your masculinity, it shouldn't bother you much to have a woman on top of you. It's a good deal more relaxing, it's often more satisfying for both parties, and you can see a lot more of what's going on. Don't get into the habit, though, or you might turn into a woosy.

Later, I picked up a hairbrush and ran it through my moss a few times in the dim reflection of the mirror on the bedroom door. My moss looked pretty much the same whether or not I brushed it. It was just sort of a private ritual with me to brush my hair before I went to bed. Life was full of things that made a lot less sense than that.

'Why do you brush your hair before you go to bed?' asked Uptown Judy.

It was a hard question and I wasn't really sure I knew the answer.

It wasn't so much a matter of vanity. I think I just wanted to be sure I was really there. With a sense of dread I considered the possibility of my not ever being there again after Wednesday night. Only a lonely hairbrush combing the cobwebs of a lonely loft.

I glanced over at the peaceful form under the covers. She was a woman lying on a bed in North America. Why burden Uptown Judy with my problems? I patted the cat and got back into bed.

'I want to make a good impression on my pillow,' I said.

45

I took the litter box and a week's supply of cat food and put them in the freight elevator. Then I ran back for the cat, and with all our travel gear, the two of us rode up to Winnie Katz's.

Ah, Isle of Lesbos. Strange and sweet are thee. Forbidden and fragile, thy charm. Forget it, sailor.

'Come in,' said a voice. I came in, closed the door, and put down the cat. Winnie was sitting at her kitchen table eating a bowl of Froot Loops and drinking Red Zinger herbal tea. A little lonely girl in a big lonely room.

'Sit down,' she said. 'It isn't often we get your kind up here.' I pretended not to understand, but I didn't think she bought it.

'Froot Loops,' she said a little disdainfully. 'A long time ago, my attitude toward men . . .' she paused. She said 'men' with more disdain than she'd said 'Froot Loops.' She ate some Froot Loops.

'A long time ago my attitude toward men was "Fuck 'em and feed 'em Froot Loops," ' she said. She glanced casually, coolly over at me.

'What's your attitude now?' I asked. I wasn't sure I wanted to know.

She sipped some Red Zinger and she took her time. Then she looked at me like I was a lamp and said, 'Feed 'em Froot Loops.'

It wasn't a healthy attitude, but it wasn't really a healthy world. Anyway, it was too late to find another place for the cat. I'd have to tough it out. I got up and walked over to the window and looked down at a limo parked next to three garbage trucks. Take me home, country roads.

'Ever been around any sisters of Sappho, Kinky?' she asked.

'No,' I said, 'but I've gone out with a lot of women who share your attitude toward Froot Loops.'

Winnie got up from the table and came over to the window.

'You're pretty straight, Kinky,' she said.

'That's why they call me Kinky,' I said.

'What do people like you call people like me?' she asked. She had a lukewarm, lesbianlike smile on her face, which I mistook for a sense of humor. 'Lesbians?' she asked. 'Dykes?'

I smiled my interdenominational ice-breaking smile. 'How about gap-lappers?' I asked.

She didn't laugh. She nodded her head a few times though, as if she understood men. Maybe lesbians were the only people who did. She was growing on me. She looked soft and small-town attractive in the morning sun from the window. I found myself empathizing with her. Maybe more. I didn't know how to say good-bye. I thought an older-brotherly farewell handshake might be in order, so I put out my hand. Winnie didn't even look at it.

She crossed both arms on her chest. The sapphic smile was back on her face.

'The cat stays,' she said. 'You go.'

46

The green-gray reptilian scales of the creature were gleaming obscenely in the reflected lights of the city. The thing seemed to be taking on a life of its own.

'Bill Dick's got a big lizard,' said Ratso. It was between sets. We were standing on the third-floor balcony of the Lone Star Cafe. I was still alive.

'Yes, he does,' I said. An involuntary shudder went through me. I'd had a few shots and I was trying to pace myself for the second show, which wasn't to start for over an hour.

'Good set,' said Larry Campbell. Campbell was arguably the best all-around musician in the city. He could play any instrument known to Western man and a few that weren't. He wasn't too excited about Dick's lizard.

'You guys were hot,' I said.

'Decent,' said Campbell. 'Decent.' Borrowing a phrase from the New York Rangers hockey players who often came to see the show. To them, everything in the world was either 'decent' or 'brutal.' Not a bad way to look at life, I thought. Tonight, I suspected, would fall into what you'd call your brutal area.

Campbell wandered back into the dressing room to talk to some young female admirers. You didn't get world-class groupies at the Lone Star. I wasn't even sure that there was such a thing. Groupies were groupies. Age, sex, area of interest didn't figure into it. Adoration was one thing, but worship was enough to bore the pants off you, sometimes literally.

It was around eleven-fifteen. Still early. It was New Year's Eve, and New York was a late town anyway. The only later ones were probably Vegas and ancient Rome. So I wasn't too worried that I hadn't seen Simmons, Flippo, or Gunner yet. They might've been there all the time. It was a mad-house downstairs. A zoo and a half. Where the hell was Rambam?

Ratso took a sip of my Molson and smiled. 'Well,' he said, 'we're halfway home.'

'Where the hell's Simmons?' I asked. 'I thought he was going to do a few songs tonight.'

'Don't worry,' said Ratso, 'he's here. Said to tell you just to call on him. He said he'd play "if the good Lord's willin' and the creek don't rise." Nice colloquialism.'

'You know who always used to say that, don't you?' I asked.

'No,' said Ratso, 'who said it?'

152

'Hank Williams used to say that at the end of his radio shows.'

'That's good,' said Ratso.

'What's so good about it?' I asked.

'I was afraid,' said Ratso as he took another sip of my Molson, 'that it might be Oscar Wilde.'

Cleve had apparently spoken to Ratso. There had been a little problem already with the two Judys. Both their names had been on the 'hit list,' and Uptown Judy, arriving first, hadn't had any trouble getting in. But when Downtown Judy arrived, the guy at the door, not a rocket scientist, had told her, 'I think you're here already.'

Downtown Judy had become somewhat perturbed. The guy at the door had called for Cleve. Cleve had called for Ratso and Ratso had shown the guy that there were two Judys on the hit list. Downtown Judy had become highly agitated then, and it was at that time that Ratso, according to himself, had applied the master's touch. He'd told her, 'Kinky didn't want you to have any problems getting in, so he put your name down twice.'

The dressing room was more frantic than a methadone clinic at closing time, and the overflow was spilling into the open-air patio. The iguana didn't look like it wanted any more company, and I knew I didn't. Except for Rambam. Where the hell was Rambam?

I tried to settle down and take stock of things. Cleve, Bill Dick, Simmons were all there, though I'd only seen Cleve. Where Flippo and Gunner were was anybody's guess. Through the door to the dressing room I saw Patrick the bouncer talking to a large, squat form by the doorway. Sergeant Cooperman. My backup unit was here. Very comforting.

I figured if I stayed in one place long enough, everybody'd

find me. Everybody. Even Hank Williams and Kaw-liga the wooden Indian. No point in going downstairs where the crowd was. It's never a good idea to mix with the crowd when you're performing, anyway. Tends to demystify you.

I was heading into the dressing room for another Molson. I'd just gotten inside the doorway when Bill Dick collared me.

'Kinkster,' said Bill Dick, 'I'd like you to meet the club's lawyer.' He introduced me to a fairly glib-looking guy with a gold chain and an Italian name Thurmon Munson couldn't've caught the first time around.

We talked for a few minutes. The guy was pretty funny for a lawyer. 'Like you to meet my wife, Mary,' he said. 'She's Irish. I'm a social climber.'

The only thing I was climbing was the walls. I was starting to get real nervous. I glanced around the dressing room. Sal Lorello, dapper former manager in from Chappaqua for the show. Nick 'Chinga' Chavin, country singer turned ad exec. Earl Shuman, music publisher and author of some great songs himself. Corky Laing, world-class rock drummer. Found him in the Congo, beatin' on his bongo.

I got the Molson and walked back outside onto the patio. Had to stay away from the hard stuff just now. Had to pace myself. Didn't want to peak too soon. I could've been thinking this way before any show. Unfortunately, tonight the subject wasn't music. It was murder.

McGovern and my brother Roger were leaning on the iguana talking with each other. McGovern had a vodka tonic balanced precariously on the third toenail of the creature's left hind foot.

'I'm here for moral support,' said Roger.

'Nothing's going to happen,' said Ratso calmly. 'Nothing's going to happen.'

McGovern didn't say anything. He didn't have to say

anything. The look on his face said that something was going to happen. And McGovern was a very accurate paranoid. Almost an idiot savant when it came to sensing danger. He looked worried as hell, and that made me worried as hell. It made it a little tough for me to be thinking what song I wanted to open the second set with.

It was cold on the patio. It was hot in the dressing room. But I was still alive.

There was always something to be said for that.

47

There wasn't much for me to do but stand around and look at the iguana like everybody else. Hell of a way to finish off the year.

But I had to stay out of trouble, as they say. 'Don't trouble trouble till trouble troubles you, Mr Hank,' like the janitor at the sanitarium told Hank Williams. Amazing how much of Flippo's book stayed with you.

I walked over to the edge of the patio where you could look over the wall onto Fifth Avenue. Headlights were hurrying down the avenue lest they be late on their pathetic way to close out the old and ring in the new. They did it every year. But there was nothing new in New York, I thought. A few new bums on the Bowery. Maybe their New Year's resolution hadn't kicked in yet from the year before. And yet, one kept hoping . . .

A shadow moved next to me.

It came close to me, reached into the folds of an overcoat, and handed me a Gideon Bible. It was Rambam.

'Got it,' he said. 'I used the old blue jeans and bucket of ice trick.'

'Oh, that one,' I said as my pulse began to slow a bit. 'What the hell's the old blue jeans and bucket of ice trick?'

'Well, you said he recently moved to the Gramercy Park. Now, if you want to get in a hotel room, you obtain the room number from the desk. I won't go into that. Anyway, you get the room number. Then you go up to the floor the room's on. You take off your shoes, socks, and shirt and leave 'em out on the stairway. You get a bucket of ice and you walk around with your blue jeans, the bucket of ice, and an embarrassed expression until you find a maid or hotel employee and you ask could they help you, you locked yourself out of your room. Works every time.'

I looked at Rambam. He was smiling. 'Never fails,' he said.

'What'd you find?' I asked.

'A fucking Hank Williams museum,' said Rambam.

'And the picture?'

From under his coat Rambam took out a room-service menu and opened it up. There was Howie's #1 BBQ, the two kids, and poor old Hank. There was the autograph and the date, December 31, 1952.

'Watcha got?' asked Ratso. Rambam quickly started to close the menu over the picture, but I stopped him.

'No harm in them seeing it.' I said. McGovern and Roger were drifting over, too. They studied the photograph.

'That's probably the last autograph he ever signed,' said McGovern.

'Might be worth a fortune,' Ratso said.

The moon was rising slowly over the Chrysler Building, and it lent an eerie quality to the old black-and-white photograph.

The children in the picture had that awkward, trapped, charming look common to the children of the fifties. Like kids in the audience on Groucho Marx or Beaver Cleaver and his friends.

'Who are the kids?' McGovern said with a laugh.

'I don't know,' I said, 'but I'm pretty sure...' My voice trailed off as I studied the photograph more closely.

'Yeah?' Ratso asked. 'What are you pretty sure about?'

'That one of these two little boys is going to try to kill me tonight.'

48

'Five minutes, Mr Jolson,' said Cleve from the door of the dressing room.

'Christ,' I said. What a hell of a way to start a year. Perform an hour show for a madhouse full of brontosaurus material while you try to avoid getting snuffed by a homicidal maniac.

I put on my Nudie's of Hollywood Jesus coat that Bob Dylan had given me. It had palm trees, rainbows, pictures of Jesus, and three crosses on the back. The two outer crosses were occupied but the middle one was empty. Either the Lord had risen or he'd gone out to get a donut. The religious significance didn't bother me, only that the damn coat was too heavy to wear onstage. Had enough sequins to choke an iguana.

I strapped on my guitar.

I walke down the long narrow hallway on the third floor. The band was already onstage, and I could hear Larry Campbell launching them into 'Exodus' and intricately weaving it into 'Spurs That Jingle Jangle Jingle.' Hell of a medley.

On the stairway to the second floor I picked up Boris and Patrick, who stayed right with me all the way to the stage. Having security not only made you feel secure, it made you feel important. Like the leader of a small African nation.

The set went extremely well. It was only forty-five minutes out of my life – fifty if you counted the encore –

and it provided pleasure and entertainment to others. I wasn't Judy Garland, but I wasn't bad.

I played all the old favorites. 'They Ain't Makin' Jews Like Jesus Anymore,' 'Get Your Biscuits in the Oven and Your Buns in the Bed,' 'The Ballad of Charles Whitman,' 'Sold American,' 'Ride 'Em Jewboy,' 'Waitress, Please Waitress, Come Sit on My Face,' 'Ol' Shep,' 'Ira Hayes,' and 'Ol' Ben Lucas.'

There was rather a poignant moment at the end of 'They Ain't Makin' Jews Like Jesus Anymore' when I brought onto the stage Lee Frazier, America's Favorite Negro, and John A. Walsh, America's Most Influential Albino, and the three of us sang harmony together. That was what I called the brotherhood-in-action segment of the show.

It was at that time that Chet Flippo made his move for the stage. Boris and Patrick T-boned him directly in front of the center mike, but all he had with him was a slip of paper with a song request on it. Boris handed it up to me. It read: 'Play "Proud to Be an Asshole from El Paso." '

I never refuse a sensitive request. I played the song. Flippo was out of it anyway. I'd known him from the time Rambam turned up with the photograph.

I called Mike Simmons up and he sang 'Your Cheatin' Heart' and several other tunes that went down well with the crowd. As Simmons left the stage he said to me, 'Got to see you right after the show.'

'Fine,' I said. I didn't mind seeing John Wayne Gacey after the show. Before the show was when I didn't want to be bummed out. Had to pace myself.

I played a few more songs, told the crowd it'd been a financial pleasure, and reminded them, if they were driving, not to forget their cars. I ended the set with 'Before All Hell Breaks Loose.'

Twenty-seven minutes later, it did.

49

Gunner was in the dressing room when I got there. She was sitting on the dilapidated couch, with her legs crossed, smoking a cigarette.

'Fine performance, Kinky,' she said.

I leaned the guitar against a wall. 'Another show in my hip pocket,' I said.

I started to take off my Jesus coat but decided against it. It might bring me some clout wherever I was going next. The rest of the band was coming into the dressing room, along with Simmons, Downtown Judy, and a few others. It had been a long night, and it wasn't over yet.

I walked out onto the patio to smoke a solitary cigar under the iguana's chin. Boris was now at the dressing room door, keeping a watchful eye on me. Funny in the music business how you're either swarmed by people or left completely alone with a cigar and an iguana. There didn't seem to be much middle ground. I once thought that being alone was superior to being alone in a crowd. Now, I didn't see that it made a hell of a lot of difference.

Maybe God was just a nice Jewish dentist, and *Time* and *Life* and *People* were only things we looked at ever so casually and briefly in his nicely furnished, antiseptic waiting room with a little Barry Antelope music piped in.

I puffed on the cigar and looked for an occasional, wayward star that might've gotten lost somewhere between Trump Tower and the World Trade Center. I found one and made a wish. One of these days maybe Jiminy Cricket will step out of the woodwork. Then, if somebody doesn't mistake him for a cockroach and crush his back, I figure I'm in business.

I went back into the now-packed dressing room, went over to my guitar case, and got out the room-service menu and the AAA road atlas. I went downstairs with Boris to find Cooperman and Fox. Before I left the dressing room Simmons asked me to meet him in an hour or so at Marylou's. I'd told him I would.

Lee Frazier unlocked the rear door to the basement for me. I stationed Boris in the executive men's room and told him that at the first sound of trouble to come on the run. Then I met Cooperman and Fox on the back stairway of the club. It was agreed that they'd keep a close surveillance on the basement and be ready for action if necessary. I walked through the basement to the manager's office and knocked on the door.

50

'Just a minute,' said a familiar voice. Then the door opened. 'Come on in,' said Cleve. 'You want to get paid?'

'That was one idea I had,' I said. We were in the little office alone. Cleve went over to the door and locked the bolt on it.

'Sit down,' he said. 'I'm still counting the cash. You made out like a bandit tonight. You got the five coming to you, and we went into percentages at the door. A real financial pleasure for you, pal.' Cleve laughed a friendly laugh.

'Music to my ears,' I said. Cleve was counting the money and I was counting imaginary worry beads and getting pretty damn nervous.

'You read Flippo's book?' I asked. I lit a cigar.

'Yeah,' said Cleve. 'He had some inaccurate shit in there, but on the whole it wasn't bad. If you're into Hank Williams.' He kept counting the cash. I kept puffing on the cigar.

'Cleve,' I said, 'give it a rest for a minute. Forget the

money. The only currency I value is the coin of the spirit. Take a look at this map, will you?'

Cleve spread the road atlas out over the desk. 'What's this for?' he asked. 'You thinking of going on a trip?'

'Not quite,' I said. 'Anything look familiar?' I pointed to the Virginia – West Virginia section – Hank's last ride.

'Yeah,' said Cleve with a little smile.

'I know,' I said. 'Chilhowie, to be exact.'

'How'd you know that?' asked Cleve, a very slight wariness creeping into his voice. The room was hot. It was also starting to feel a hell of a lot smaller than when I first walked in. My eyes went quickly, almost unconsciously, to the bolt on the door, a gesture that didn't go unnoticed by Cleve.

'You can thank Mick Brennan for it,' I said. 'He put his beer down on top of my road atlas last Saturday night at the Monkey's Paw. That's how Howie's #1 BBQ got to be Chilhowie's #1 BBQ.'

'Very clever,' said Cleve. 'Go on.' The color was beginning to go from his face, and there hadn't been all that much there to begin with. A nerve was twitching under his left eye.

'The time frame was right,' I said. 'You were there when Hank passed through on his way to Canton, Ohio. When I asked you about it earlier you told me you were an only child. Then you said, "We grew up in Kentucky." I remembered that and it sounded strange. So I called the courthouse at the county seat and I found the court records concerning your dead brother, Joe. Died two days after Hank Williams died. Hank was twenty-nine. Joe was ten. You were twelve. That about right?'

The twitch under Cleve's eye was getting worse. 'That's ancient history,' he said in a half whisper, half croak. He was staring at Chilhowie on the map, and his eye was twitching. It wasn't getting better. The whole left eye was twitching at two-second intervals. Looked like a method actor practicing a lascivious wink in front of a mirror.

'That may be ancient history,' I said, 'but this isn't.' I flipped the Gramercy Park room-service menu with the photo inside that Rambam had lifted onto Cleve's desk. 'This was taken from your hotel room about three hours ago,' I said in a cold, deliberate voice. 'Want anything from room service?'

He opened the menu with all the forethought of a trained chimp. He sat there rigid, staring through the photo. His brother, himself, and old Hank stared timelessly, effortlessly back at him.

'Picture from life's other side,' I said. Cleve was trembling. Whether from fear, rage, or eleven different herbs and spices I couldn't be sure. I didn't stick around to find out. I went to the door and grabbed the bolt. It didn't budge. I heard a desk drawer open. 'Boris!' I shouted. 'Boris!'

I turned around. The photo, the road atlas, hundred-dollar bills were falling through the air seemingly in slow motion like a one-man ticker-tape parade, and through the ticker tape, like a cadaver in high gear, came Cleve directly for me. In his left hand, sickeningly, yet predictably, was a tomahawk.

51

When I regained consciousness, it was in a hospital bed. Like a guy swimming underwater, I could feel myself gradually coming to the surface. First, I heard voices, but the words were unintelligible. One voice had a New Yorky, rodentlike quality to it that seemed faintly familiar.

The first images I saw were two blurred figures standing by a window. When they came into clearer focus, I saw that it was Ratso and a doctor engaged in some kind of a discussion. The doctor, apparently, was explaining something, and Ratso was nodding his head very somberly. His serious demeanor was not especially comforting.

The first actual words I heard the doctor say to Ratso were, 'A tomahawk wound in the groin can be a very serious thing if it isn't treated promptly.' I lost consciousness again.

When I came to for the second time, Ratso was sitting on the bed eating a pastrami sandwich about the size of his head and I was in great pain. 'Congratulations,' Ratso said, 'you're a hero.'

I didn't feel like a hero. I also didn't feel like watching a man do unnatural things to a pastrami sandwich two feet away from my head. I tried to look heroic.

'Very clever, Sherlock,' said Ratso between bites, 'that Chilhowie business. But how'd you know to look back that far in time for the motive?'

'My dear Ratso,' I said, 'the pattern became fairly obvious early on. Take a look at Hank's victims. What do you see?'

'Okay,' said Ratso. 'We've got Larry Barkins, Bubba Borgelt, and Ned Glaser. They were all country singers and they all had the poor judgment to play the Lone Star Cafe.'

'There's something more, Ratso,' I said. 'It's so obvious that it's easy to miss. It's why I invited Roger down for the show and made sure Cleve knew about it.

'You see, by this time I knew that Cleve was Hank. And, as Hank, I knew that he was not just killing country singers. He was killing *brothers*.'

Ratso stared at me. He stopped eating his sandwich.

'I first saw the pattern,' I said, 'after Bubba Borgelt bought it. But I became even more sure when Hank spared the Burrito Brothers.

'Cleve was clearly one of the little boys in the Chilhowie photograph. He was in the right place at the right time. The real Hank Williams died sometime during the night on the same date the photograph was taken.'

'Then that autograph really was authentic?' asked Ratso.

'Of course not,' I said. 'It was forged by Cleve. Another small step on the way to his assuming the Hank identity. In 1952 there was no way any photograph could've been developed in time for the real Hank to have signed it.'

'Of course not,' said Ratso.

'Two days after Hank Williams died, Cleve's younger brother Joe died. This is in the courthouse records. Whether Cleve blamed himself for his brother's death or actually killed him requires further investigation. One thing is for sure, however: He was not his brother's keeper.'

'Truly amazing, Sherlock,' said Ratso, 'but I still don't understand one thing. Why would Hank spare the Burrito Brothers?'

'Because those brothers aren't really brothers,' I said. 'A rudimentary knowledge of country music always helps.'

'Yeah,' said Ratso. He stared at the ruins of his pastrami sandwich. 'It's amazing I've gotten this far in life without it.'

'Look at it this way,' I said. 'If we ever run into a case involving Jesus, Bob Dylan, or Hitler, we're all set.'

Ratso laughed. 'You never know,' he said.

52

Several days later I was feeling much better when Ratso came in with the newspapers, the mail, and a large number of Pete Myers' pork pies from Myers of Keswick.

'I can't believe the great press you're still getting,' said Ratso. 'McGovern is really having a ball with this. If you'll pardon the expression.'

'How's Cleve?' I asked.

'Well,' said Ratso, 'aside from the fact that he thinks he's

164

Hank full-time now and that his face is jumping around like a flea circus, he's doing all right.'

'That's good to know,' I said.

'The shrinks are giving him a thorough checkup from the neck up, but even his voice and his mannerisms have drastically altered. He keeps telling them he's got to move on. He's got a show to do, he says. No doubt about it, Kinkster, the boy's got a fan belt loose.'

'What's in the mail?' I asked, grimacing slightly as I got up on my elbows. I still couldn't quite sit up in bed.

'Here's a nice note from Flippo. His book's gone into a second printing, largely thanks to you, he says.'

'Anytime,' I said.

'Here's a highly unusual photo of you that Gunner sent.' Ratso passed the photo over to me. It was a shot of me sitting on a barstool looking rather dazed.

'Good publicity shot,' I said. 'Anything else you'd like to share with the whole class?'

'Well,' said Ratso, 'this is a little strange. It's a large manila envelope. Big block letters on it.'

'Open it,' I said.

Ratso opened the envelope and handed me the contents. It was the sheet music to the Hank Williams song 'I Can't Help It If I'm Still in Love with You.'

There was a note attached. It read: 'I'll always cherish the time we spent together. Let's do it again real soon. All my love, Judy.'

Ratso grabbed it out of my hands and looked it over. 'That's very sweet of her,' he said. 'You definitely ought to call her or drop her a line.'

'Can't,' I said.

'Why not?' Ratso asked.

'I don't know if it's Uptown or Downtown,' I said.

I took out one of the cigars Ratso had smuggled into the room for me and lit it up.

'Look, Ratso,' I said, 'I'm almost afraid to ask, but there's one more thing.'

'What is it?' Ratso asked.

'Did you save the Jesus coat?'

'Don't worry,' he said. 'It's safe in a closet – in my apartment.' I leaned back on the pillows and took a lazy puff on the cigar.

'You're like a brother to me, Ratso,' I said.